# His Forbidden Bride

# By Merry Farmer

**HIS FORBIDDEN BRIDE**

Copyright ©2016 by Merry Farmer

Cover design by Erin Dameron-Hill (the miracle-worker)
Embellishment by © Olgasha | Dreamstime.com

ASIN: B01LD2PWBK
Paperback:
ISBN-13: 9781537416953

ISBN-10: 1537416952

If you'd like to be the first to learn about when the next books in the series come out and more, please sign up for my newsletter here: http://eepurl.com/RQ-KX

Like historical western romance? Come join us in the Pioneer Hearts group on Facebook for games, prizes, exclusive content, and first looks at the latest releases of your favorite historical western authors. https://www.facebook.com/groups/pioneerhearts/

**For L.M. Montgomery**

Yep, I'm dedicating a book
to one of my all-time favorite authors.

Mostly because I borrowed something from her for the
plot of this book. ;)

# Table of Contents

# Chapter One

*Haskell, Wyoming – 1876*

Honoria Bonneville was about to go mad. The clock on the mantel of Dr. Abernathy's office ticked with such deep foreboding that it pulled every nerve in her body taut. She wrung her white handkerchief in her hands as she sat hunched in a spindly chair on the other side of the waiting room from the clock. Her lungs burned, but she fought the urge to cough—fought it and fought it and fought it until she couldn't hold out anymore.

She burst into a spell of coughing that wracked her from head to toe and made the pale, middle-aged woman sitting across from her start. That woman quickly fell into coughing too, as if Honoria's outburst were contagious. A third patient—an older man—frowned and hugged himself tightly, as if summoning the willpower to not be made sick by the women. Honoria squeezed her eyes shut, praying for her lungs to be still.

Heaven knew she had enough practice holding her breath and keeping the things that were inside of her from coming out. She'd been biting her tongue and swallowing all of the things she had wanted to say for the past twenty-five years of incessant bullying by her sisters, Vivian and Melinda. She'd even endured snide comments and a turned-up nose from her younger sister, Bebe.

Once upon a time, she'd tried to speak out, to fight back against the unfairness that was heaped on her. It had been easier when she was a small girl and her mother was still alive. Ariana Bonneville had been the one light of hope in young Honoria's life. She had been the single stabilizing influence in Rex Bonneville's life—though he'd never appreciated her for it. She'd been the center of Honoria's world, and when she'd died in childbirth— along with Rex Bonneville's only son—when Honoria was seven, the light had gone out of her world. And the sense had gone out of the Bonneville family.

Grief that had never healed spilled through Honoria, and she dissolved into another round of wracking coughs that brought tears to her eyes. It was the coughing that made her cry, she insisted to herself, not grief, not pity for her lot in life. As her mother lay dying, her final words to Honoria had been, "Always remember who you are, Honoria. Your honor is your shining light. Hold your head up high, face your trials bravely, and be honest in all things." There had been words of love and sorrow too, but in every day that passed since then, Honoria had obeyed her mother, behaved with quiet honor, and born the brutality of her sisters and the neglect of her father with as much courage and strength as she could muster...for Mother's sake.

Now that strength was failing her. She coughed again, in unison with the other woman waiting to see Dr. Abernathy. She'd been strong as long as she could, but for months now Honoria had felt the unmistakable sensation of the Universe holding its breath. Something was about to change.

The door to Dr. Abernathy's examination room swung open, and Dr. Abernathy himself popped his head into the waiting room. He held a small stack of files that he looked at several times between staring at Honoria, the old man, and the other woman. He shuffled through the papers in the file, cleared his throat, then focused on Honoria.

"With a cough like that, I'd better see you first."

An unexpected tremor of fear passed through Honoria as she stood and slipped across the waiting room to the examination room. Dr. Abernathy stood back so she could go before him. Once she was inside, hovering anxiously beside a short table, Dr. Abernathy shut the door.

"Let's see now." Dr. Abernathy shuffled through the files, mumbling to himself. He set one down on the table, then scowled as he thumbed through the other two. "What an utter nuisance."

"I'm sorry?" Honoria asked in a small voice.

Dr. Abernathy made a disapproving noise. "Why does Dr. Meyers keep insisting on seeing patients when he is constantly being called out to that blasted Indian reservation?"

Honoria blinked, unsure if she was supposed to answer the question. "I saw Dr. Meyers about my cough this morning." She opted to explain.

"Yes, and I'm sure your father will have something to say about that," Dr. Abernathy grumbled. "I've been your family doctor for years."

There was no point in explaining that that was the exact reason she'd seen someone else about her concerns. "Dr. Meyers had just finished examining me—listening to my lungs, testing my sputum with some chemicals he has—when the army officer came to take him to the Cheyenne camp. I…I understand it was an emergency."

Dr. Abernathy continued to mutter, "Damned inconvenient, if you ask me. Causing me extra work. Those savages don't deserve it."

A sudden snap of dislike caught Honoria off-guard, sending her into another coughing fit.

At last, Dr. Abernathy set one of the two files he held aside and his expression lightened. "Ah! Here we are. Just as I suspected." His countenance turned grave. He stared at her over the top of his glasses. Honoria began to shake, too afraid to ask what he suspected. She didn't have to ask. "It's obvious, really," he went on. "Consumption."

Honoria's breath caught in her throat, and the room went dark for a moment. Her legs turned to jelly, and if she hadn't reached out to grab the examination table, she was certain she would have fallen over. She'd known it. In her heart, she'd known all along. And she knew what consumption was.

It was a death sentence.

"Looks like it's fairly advanced, going by Dr. Meyers's notes," Dr. Abernathy went on, as if describing how a garden wall was built. "The coughing will continue, as will instances of coughing up blood. Yes, yes." He scanned the rest of the file. "I wouldn't plan on lasting more than six months to a year."

"That's it?" Honoria squeaked, clutching her handkerchief to her chest.

Dr. Abernathy shrugged. "Could be less, could be more." He cleared his throat and closed the file, tossing it on the table with the others. "If I were you, young woman, I would get my affairs in order."

The tears that had stung Honoria's eyes earlier

burned hotter. That was it? Twenty-five years and her life was over? She shook her head, her shoulders sinking. Twenty-five years of life and what did she have to show for it? A battered spirit and an empty heart.

What a waste. What a terrible, terrible waste.

Dr. Abernathy cleared his throat. "I have other patients to see. More than usual, thanks to Dr. Meyers."

Honoria blinked up at him through her shock and grief. That was all he had to say? Censure for Dr. Meyers? After giving her a death sentence? The urge to run filled her.

"Thank you for your time, sir." She managed to push out the words with a hoarse breath.

Dr. Abernathy grunted, then pivoted to hold the door open for her. Clutching her handkerchief to her chest, Honoria hurried out the door. She tried to hold her head high—like she always did—as she made her way through the waiting room, but as soon as she was out in the hot, July sun of Haskell, she burst into bitter, wrenching tears.

Consumption. Death. Emptiness. Her heart tried to soar up to wherever her mother was, longing to be with her now instead of after months of bitter, painful decline. Because what did she have to look forward to in the few, short months remaining to her? She certainly wouldn't get any sympathy from her father. He barely noticed her as it was. Papa didn't like illness. He would shunt her off to some back room in the house and pretend she wasn't there.

Blindly, Honoria walked away from Dr. Abernathy's office, up Prairie Avenue. Being ignored by her father was the least of her worries. Her sisters would be furious. Yes, furious. They would resent every last moment of Honoria's life. They were losing their chief servant, after all. Honoria wasn't fool enough to think they would show her a moment's sympathy. Oh no, they would likely try to pry as much work out of her for as long as they could, making her sew through her coughing. Vivian was marrying Cousin Rance in less than a week, and already Honoria was being worked until she dropped on the wedding gown and Vivian's trousseau. How much more work would be demanded of her before she dropped?

The horrible thought propelled her forward. She picked up her pace, shivering as she ran past the houses of so many people who could have been her friends if she'd only had the strength to break away from her family. Why hadn't she shown some backbone and befriended them all while she had the chance? Had she misinterpreted her mother's dying wish that she be strong and have honor? It was too late now. Her life was over. Her pitiful, wasted life.

"Honoria, what's wrong?"

The question came from Elspeth Strong, whose house Honoria was running past. Some sort of garden party was going on at the Strong house. Seeing so many happy people was like an arrow in Honoria's heart. But before Honoria could rush on, Elspeth caught up to her and laid a hand on her arm.

Honoria stumbled, then spun toward Elspeth. The pain of her wasted life was too much in the face of such a friendly gesture. Honoria had risked her family's wrath to help Elspeth and Athos and their children several weeks ago. Maybe she could turn to Elspeth for comfort now.

Trembling, she launched herself into Elspeth's arms, hugging her like the friend she could have had if she'd been braver. It was too late now.

"What's wrong?" Elspeth asked, deep concern in her voice.

Sense hit Honoria, and she pulled away. She couldn't

lay her troubles at Elspeth's doorstep. It wasn't right. Instead, she turned this way and that, looking up and down the street for answers. There were none anywhere. She started to leave, then hung back, no idea what to do.

Her illness spoke for her, and before she could stop it, a bout of wracking coughs nearly doubled her over. She started crying all over again, sick at heart and ashamed of her weakness.

"Oh dear." Elspeth rushed to hug her. The gesture was far more welcome than Elspeth would ever know, as was her plea of, "Please, please tell me what's wrong, Honoria."

"I…I…" Honoria hid her face against Elspeth's shoulder. It would have been so wonderful to have a friend. It may have been too late for much of a friendship, but perhaps she could risk one confidence. Head still resting against Elspeth's shoulder, she whispered, "I'm dying."

Elspeth tensed. "What? No, there must be some mistake."

"Elspeth?"

When Elspeth twisted to answer her husband Athos's questioning call, Honoria broke out of her arms. She couldn't lay this burden on anyone else's shoulders. No one else should bear this but her. There was no time left to find consolation in friendship, no time left for—

She gasped as she glanced past Elspeth's shoulder to Athos. He wasn't the only one approaching. Following hard on his heels was Solomon Templesmith.

Honoria's heart lurched in her chest, twisting with longing and grief. Solomon Templesmith, Haskell's banker, one of the wealthiest men in town. He was tall and strode toward her with purpose. His expensive, tailored suit fit his broad shoulders perfectly. His chocolate skin stood out against his white collar and cuffs. His dark, dreamy eyes held deep concern for her. They always did, every time he'd been there to catch her when she tripped or to smile at her when everyone else was frowning. Her father despised Solomon with every fiber of his being, despised that a man who had been born a slave could have as much money and as high of a standing in Haskell society as he did.

Honoria had loved him since the moment she first laid eyes on his kind, world-weary face and heard his rich sonorous voice.

Solomon Templesmith would have to watch her die now.

No, worse than that, she would have to die locked far, far away from him, where she would never see his kind eyes or feel his strong arms around her again.

She couldn't bear the thought. Before he could reach her, she turned and ran away down Prairie Avenue.

She made it almost all the way to the intersection with Elizabeth Street before hearing Solomon's concerned call of, "Honoria, stop!"

She could only manage a few more, tripping steps before lurching to a halt. Rough coughing stopped her. She shouldn't be running, as sick as she was. She held her handkerchief to her mouth, helpless to do anything but wait until Solomon caught up with her.

"Honoria, my God." He skipped straight past politeness and gripped her arms as he reached her.

Honoria's coughing subsided, and she let her hand fall from her mouth. "I…" She couldn't meet his eyes, could only stare down at the contrast between her white handkerchief and the dark brown skin of his hands. "I…" She couldn't. She couldn't burden him.

Only, before she could summon up the strength to

break free from his supporting hands, Solomon said, "Elspeth told me what you said to her."

Honoria snapped her eyes up to meet his, full of fear. Would he reject her now? The one person she admired above all else?

No, there was so much tenderness, so much regret in his eyes that all she could do was break down into sobs and nod.

"No," he whispered.

And right there, in broad daylight, directly across from the hotel, near one of the busiest intersections in Haskell, Solomon Templesmith pulled her into a tight embrace, resting her head against his shoulder. No one, not even her own father, would ever show her so much sympathy. Solomon was little more than a stranger, forbidden in so many ways, but the comfort he was offering turned her inside out and made her feel as though she was floating in the midst of her misery. She wept freely against him, leaning heavily into the firm muscles of his chest, closing her arms around his back. She'd dreamed of this moment with him for years, only to have it come at the end.

They might have stood there for hours or it might have only been seconds when Solomon said, "Tell me all about it."

Sense returned to her slowly. She gulped a few breaths, working to have the power to stand on her own. As soon as she could, she pushed back, wiping away her tears and straightening her back. It still took several deep, deliberate breaths before she could raise her gaze to meet his.

"Dr. Abernathy says I have consumption," she admitted, her voice shaking like tall grass in a storm. "He says I have months left."

Solomon's expression crumpled into extreme sympathy. "Oh, Honoria, I'm so sorry."

He could have left her right there, but instead he took her hand and led her over to the side of the road, to a bench that sat out in front of Charlie and Olivia Garrett's house. He helped her to sit, then sat beside her. Out of the corner of her eyes, Honoria spotted several people looking on curiously, including Mr. Gunn on the hotel's porch. She didn't mind his observation, but she wished everyone else would disappear. She wished everyone in the world but her and Solomon would disappear.

"What precisely did Dr. Abernathy say?" Solomon asked in a solid, businesslike voice.

Honoria wrung her handkerchief, used it to dabbed her eyes, and gathered her thoughts. Solomon was sitting too close to her, but at that moment she truly didn't care.

"I…I've had this cough for quite some time," she began in a weak and weary voice. "Bonnie—you know, Bonnie Horner, who's walking out with my father—has been urging me to see a doctor."

"Bonnie is a wise woman." Solomon nodded.

Honoria managed a small smile for praise of the woman who—in spite of having her father for a beau—was vilified more often than not in the Bonneville house.

Her smile faded fast. "I went to see Dr. Meyers first thing this morning. He examined me. He even ran a test with chemicals that he explained were new and helped diagnose disease." Solomon made an impressed sound. "But he was called away by an army officer. Dr. Abernathy takes over his cases when Dr. Meyers is away, so I left and went about my business until this afternoon." She sniffled as recent, bad memories assailed her. "I went to Dr. Abernathy for the results just now, and he told me."

She squeezed her eye shut, and more tears streamed down her face.

"Could Dr. Abernathy have been wrong?" Solomon asked.

Honoria shook her head. "He had Dr. Meyers's file. I saw Dr. Meyers writing in that file while he was examining me."

Solomon's shoulder sagged. "I'm so sorry." He rubbed Honoria's back, sliding his arm around her and letting her rest her head on his shoulder from the side.

"My life has been such a waste," she blurted before she could stop herself. Her tears continued to spill.

"Don't say that." Solomon's voice was so tender that it only made her weep harder.

"But it's true. I've let myself be pushed around and bullied by my sisters since Mama died. I've lived a half-life. And there were so many things I wanted to do."

"What did you want to do?" He brushed a loose strand of hair away from her forehead.

Honoria sighed, closing her eyes. "I wanted to make something of myself. I wanted to do something with my skills, help people. I…I wanted to fall in love, marry, and have children." Her voice faded to a wisp as she mourned all of the children she'd never have now.

"I'm sorry," he said again, covering her hands with one of his large ones.

Some people would have been horrified at the contrast of his dark skin with her pale skin, but she didn't mind. She saw his differences as something beautiful. He was so, so different from the stilted, pitiful life she'd led. In fact, Solomon represented everything she'd longed for but would never have now—newness, enterprise, carving paths through life in ways that never would have been permitted little more than a decade ago. Solomon was the strength and bravery her mother had wished for her to have.

"Are you afraid of dying?" he asked in a hushed voice after they'd been silent for a while.

Honoria held still as she thought, then shook her head. "I'm afraid of what these last few months of my life will be like," she confessed. She was suddenly filled with the certainty that she could say anything to Solomon, anything at all.

"Your family." He sighed, proving that he understood. He squeezed her hands.

"I know this is cruel to say, but I don't think they'll care," she admitted, barely over a whisper. "Vivian and Melinda will be put out because they're losing their drudge."

He didn't contradict her. He didn't censure her. He didn't try to convince her that she was wrong, that they would care. He just let her speak, and he listened.

"Papa will be embarrassed that someone of his stock could be so weak. He'll…he'll say I take after my mother, that it's her fault. I can't stand it when he speaks badly of her." She hadn't realized how true that was until the words were out of her mouth. The very idea filled her with anger.

"I've always figured that you took after your mother." Solomon spoke calmly, a balm to Honoria's soul. "You certainly aren't like the rest of them." He paused, then said, "I wish I could have met her."

Honoria lifted her head from his shoulder and met his eyes. There was nothing but genuine compassion in their dark depths. "I wish you could have met her too."

Something wild and dangerous and spoken in her mother's voice tickled at the back of her mind. How wonderful it would have been if Honoria had been granted time to get to know Solomon better? Yes, he was a different race from her, but Wendy had married Travis, in spite of the differences in their races. Before that, Graham Tremaine had married Estelle. What was impossible in other places was more than possible in Haskell. If only there had been time. Her life would have ended so differently if she had found out the truth as Solomon's wife instead of the lonely, bullied, neglected daughter of—

Her thoughts stopped, and she gasped as the idea grabbed hold of her. Could she? She had so very little time left, but maybe…maybe it was enough.

"What?" Solomon asked, confusion furrowing his brow.

Suddenly anxious, she inched away from him. He kept hold of her hands, though. That gesture had her heart beating faster. Could she do this? Could she really entertain such a wild idea?

She angled her body toward him so that she could face him more directly. "You asked me if I was afraid to die."

"I did." He nodded, seriousness filling his features.

"And I told you I was more afraid to live the way I have been living for my last days." He nodded, encouraging her to go on. "I…I had so many hopes and dreams, and they're all dashed now. But maybe…" She began to shake. There was no way she was brave enough or bold enough to do this.

But the alternative was too horrible to think about. She drew in a long breath, squared her shoulders, and locked eyes with Solomon.

"Would you…would you be willing to marry me?" Her head spun as the words shot out, and she thought she might pass out.

"Marry you?" Solomon stared at her in wonder.

"I can't bear to waste away, locked in a room in my father's house for the last few days of my life," she rushed on while she still had courage. She clutched both of Solomon's hands with hers. "I want to have just a few months to live the life that I could have had. I…I want a tiny shred of happiness before I die."

He watched her, unblinking. At last, he took a breath and said, "It will be hard. Folks will *not* like to see a white woman marry a black man."

Honoria shook her head, blood racing through her veins with newfound excitement. "It won't matter," she insisted. "It won't be a long marriage anyhow. I'll…I'll be dead before they can work up too much of a fuss." She lowered her eyes as a twist of grief tied her stomach in knots. "You won't be burdened with me for long."

"No." He slipped a hand under her chin and raised her face until she met his eyes again. "Honoria, you could *never* be a burden to me."

She swallowed, a different kind of tears stinging at her eyes.

"I'm only afraid that I'll cause more trouble for you than you deserve," he went on.

"How could you?" she choked. "My life is already far more troubled than you could dare to dream. I want to end it with a smile, knowing that at least someone cared for me."

His expression filled with something so close to heartache that it took Honoria's breath away. Her entire existence and her one, tiny chance for happiness boiled down to whatever answer he would give her. She'd never wanted anything so badly in her life.

And yet, all he did was stare at her, watch her with such intensity that she could practically see the debate going on inside of him.

Then, after what seemed like an eternity, Solomon nodded.

Honoria let out a breath and nearly crumpled as the tension she'd been holding dispersed.

"But you have to let me ask you," he said, closing his hands around hers.

"Oh?" Quivers of excitement ran through her.

"It's only right if I ask you," he went on. Purpose filled his countenance. "Could you meet me back here tomorrow, perhaps?"

"I…" It would be a challenge to get away from the ranch with Vivian's wedding only days away. "I'll do whatever it takes to get here."

Solomon nodded, breaking into a smile. "I want to propose to you properly, Honoria. Even…even if our union will be a short one."

"Either way, you'll make me the happiest woman alive." Her voice cracked on that final word. A tiny part of her broke free from the grief that had all but consumed her. That tiny part didn't want to die quietly. It didn't want to die at all. But she would accept what fate had in store for her as long as she could have a few, short days of happiness as Solomon's wife.

# *Chapter Two*

Solomon was not a drinking man, but a fortifying whiskey at Sam Standish's saloon, The Silver Dollar, seemed in order, considering what he was about to do. He sat at the quiet end of the bar, rolling the small shot glass Sam had poured for him ten minutes ago between his fingers as he stared into nothing. Or rather, as he stared into the bittersweet decision that had faced him all day.

He'd made a promise. A promise to be a husband. A promise to be a widower. That last bit hurt more than he ever would have expected it to. Because if anyone in Haskell, Wyoming—in the entire nation, the entire world—could have tempted him to give up his determined bachelorhood, it would have been Honoria Bonneville.

He sighed and set his half-full glass on the bar-top. Sam raised a brow at him from the other side of the counter, where he'd been keeping a close eye on him, but Solomon shook his head.

Honoria Bonneville. The mere thought of her name filled him with a protective pride that he couldn't account for. There had been long, lonely nights when he would close his eyes and the vision of her sweet face, her wise and weary blue eyes, her honey-gold hair, and the troubled blush on her porcelain cheeks would keep him awake. Too many times he'd stood by while her sisters mistreated her or her father dismissed her. Each opportunity he'd had to come to her aid in the past few years had left him aching to do more for her, to be more for her. But he knew too well who he was and who she was. He knew it would be impossible at best, devastating at worst, for him to make the advances he'd wanted to make.

Until now.

Until she made the first move.

"You look like a man with a terrible weight on his shoulders." The words and the slap on the back that came with them were delivered by none other than Howard Haskell. Howard wore his usual jovial grin and carried himself as though he owned not just most of Haskell, but the world with it. Theophilus Gunn stood just behind Howard, studying Solomon with concerned curiosity, arms crossed, stroking his chin.

There never had been any point in hiding things from Howard or Gunn. If not for Howard, Solomon would probably still be a frustrated, resentful clerk struggling to prove himself to a world that didn't want anything to do with him.

"Not the weight of the world," he corrected, hooking his foot around the rung of the bar stool next to him and pulling it out for Howard to sit. Gunn sat as well. "The weight of a woman."

Both Howard and Gunn hummed with understanding and sympathy.

"Have you finally set your sights on one of the fine

ladies of our good town?" Howard puffed his chest and smiled as though it was the most fabulous idea he'd heard all day.

"Could I hazard a guess at the lady in question?" Gunn added.

Solomon sent them both a weary smile that said he knew that they knew the only woman he could possibly be talking about. At the same time, he questioned how much of Honoria's troubles were his to share with others.

He waited until Howard and Gunn were bristling with impatient curiosity, then sighed and answered, "Honoria Bonneville asked me to marry her."

Both Howard and Gunn sat straighter and gaped at him. Sam, who was on his way over—presumably to see if Howard and Gunn were thirsty—caught the statement as well, and his jaw dropped. "Well, hell, Solomon," he said. "If I'd known that was what you've been sitting here brooding about for the past half hour, I would have given you a double."

Solomon managed a short laugh for his friend. "Not sure it would help. Something tells me I need to keep a clear head for this one."

"What precisely did she say?" Gunn asked. "I mean, Honoria Bonneville is a lovely woman, but she's the last person I'd expect to make such a bold declaration."

Solomon winced and rubbed a long-fingered hand over his face. "She had good reason to approach me the way she did." That was as far as he would explain her business.

"Well...I...that is..." Howard was rarely at a loss for words, but he fumbled his way through his reply before giving up and shrugging. "Will wonders never cease?"

"Probably not," Solomon answered.

The four men continued at a loss for words before

Sam said, "Well, you've had a soft spot for Honoria for a while now, haven't you?"

Solomon nodded in affirmation and picked up his whiskey glass. He still didn't drink, though. "I've never admired any woman the way I admire Honoria," he admitted. "She is like a beacon of light in the midst of the dark ocean of the Bonneville family. She holds her head up high, even as the rest of them try to tear her down. She could have turned against them or hurled accusations that would make even their supporters think twice, I'm sure, but she has maintained her dignity and loyalty."

"Even when she shouldn't have," Gunn added.

Solomon acknowledged the comment with a sigh.

"I tell you, I don't know how a wolf like Bonneville ended up with a lamb like Honoria," Sam said, shaking his head and pouring three more shots of whiskey, though no one had asked for them.

"Honoria takes after her mother," Howard informed him with a sage nod, picking up the glass Sam slid across the bar to him. "Ariana Bonneville was a woman among women. It's a bitter shame that she died so young."

Gunn hummed as if he agreed. Once again, Solomon wished he'd met Honoria's mother.

"So what made Honoria up and ask you to marry her out of the blue like that?" Sam asked, then threw back his whiskey.

Solomon rolled his glass in his hand before answering, "She's desperate to be rescued." That wouldn't give too much away. It also didn't answer Sam's question or the curiosity in the others' eyes. He side-stepped whatever further questions they would ask by saying, "To tell you the truth, I've considered rescuing her—or courting her, at least—many times before this."

"I've always wondered why you didn't," Howard said, sipping his whiskey.

Solomon fixed him with a frank stare. "I was born into slavery, Howard. True, I was given my freedom before the war, but the color of my skin makes me a marked man in the eyes of the majority of people in this country, this world. Rex Bonneville resents me for my success, detests me for what he considers my 'uppityness.' I've always held back because of the trouble I know I would cause for Honoria. She deserves better than to constantly be the subject of derision and disgust."

Howard humphed in disagreement. "She's already the subject of derision and disgust by her own family, if you ask me."

"And in her current situation, she has no protector to shield her from it," Gunn added.

A prick of guilt struck Solomon at the thought. "So you think I should have asked her to walk out with me sooner?"

As quick as Howard and Gunn had been to reassure him seconds before, they hesitated now. It was Sam who stepped in and said, "I take it since she asked you, you said yes?"

Howard and Gunn glanced from Sam to Solomon as though neither of them had thought to ask the obvious.

Solomon nodded and took a sip of his whiskey at last. It burned going down the same way this entire situation did. "I told her that I wanted to propose to her properly."

His friends nodded in consideration. "Seems like the right thing to do," Howard said.

"I'm on my way to do it now," Solomon added.

Their brows went up and their eyes widened.

"Don't tell me you're here because you've got cold

feet," Sam said. "She asked you. The way I figure, the time for cold feet is long past."

Solomon shook his head and checked his pocket watch. "I've got another fifteen minutes until the time we said we'd meet."

"Ah." Howard put on a solemn countenance. "Engagement by arrangement."

Solomon barely had time to smirk at the comment before Gunn asked, "What would lead Honoria to ask you to marry her?" with a puzzled frown.

There was no way to continue to evade the question, so Solomon simply said, "It's not my secret to share."

The others hummed and nodded as if they understood. "Must be something big," Sam figured. A new patron had just come into the bar, so he was forced to move away from the conversation.

"Well." Howard slapped the bar when the silence had gone on too long. "I wish you the greatest marital felicity for many, many years to come."

It took everything Solomon had not to wince at the statement. Many years was far more than he could hope for. What would his friends say if they knew he was walking into a situation that was guaranteed to break his heart?

"When's the wedding?" Howard asked on. "I'd be honored to stand up with you, if you'd allow me."

"Thanks, Howard." Solomon smiled and reached out to shake Howard's hand. "We haven't set a date yet, but it'll be a matter of days."

Gunn's thoughtful frown deepened. "She asks you, and then the marriage takes place within days?" His gaze came out of its distant look and focused on Solomon. "She's not *in trouble*, is she?"

"Absolutely not," Solomon answered without

hesitation. Honoria wasn't that kind of girl. In fact, it begged the question of whether Honoria wanted to marry him to take shelter in his house for her final days or whether she hoped to take comfort in his bed. The thought delighted and unnerved him.

"Hmm." Gunn rubbed his chin. Solomon could practically see the wheels turning in Gunn's brain, and when Gunn's brain started working on a problem, the whole world was best to be on high alert. It would be much easier to confess the truth to the man, but again, it wasn't Solomon's secret to tell.

He rapped the bar-top with his knuckles, then slipped off his stool. "I need to be on my way," he told his friends.

"Best of luck." Howard slapped him on the back. "It's an odd situation, but I'm here to help you in any way."

"As am I," Gunn promised.

Solomon left the saloon feeling that he was lucky to have such remarkable friends. Because no matter how supportive they were, he knew the truth of things. A black man simply did not marry a sweet, blond-haired, blue-eyed daughter of a wealthy rancher without dire consequences. But for Honoria, he was willing to face those consequences and shelter her from them.

Honoria paced back and forth in front of the spreading maple tree at the end of Elizabeth Street, just outside of the Haskell town limits, where she and Solomon had agreed to meet that evening. It had taken a supreme effort of will to pen the note setting the time and place for their meeting that morning and to entrust it to the Bonneville family's maid, Maria, to deliver. She'd arrived at the tree early and kept to the shadows as the sun stretched toward the mountains on the western horizon, but every unexpected sound and every passing wagon made her jump out of her skin. Skin that her father would flay off of her if he caught her doing what she was about to do.

She couldn't believe what she was about to do. Up until that moment in Dr. Abernathy's office the day before, she had only been bold enough to break free from the chains of family obligation in her dreams. Even now, a huge part of her itched to turn and run, to accept her fate and face death meekly. Was it really worth the risk to steal so little time?

"Honoria?"

She jumped at the sound of Solomon's voice and whipped around to face him. Her heart thundered in her chest and she held her breath as she watched him stride nearer. The rays of the sunset made his chocolate skin as rich and warm as mahogany. His serious expression was full of strength and filled her with confidence. Yes, yes, this was worth every ounce of risk.

"Solomon," she answered him with a tremor in her voice. She couldn't help but smile as he slowed and studied her in his last few steps into the shade of the maple tree.

"You look lovely tonight."

His compliment brought a hot blush to Honoria's cheeks. She touched a hand to her hair. On a wild whim, she'd worn it down. She'd put on one of her favorite summer dresses as well. This was the only proposal she was ever going to get, she'd dreamed of it several times, asleep and awake, in the midst of the tragedy of her life, and she was going to make it as perfect as she could.

"You look very handsome yourself." She returned the compliment with lowered eyes, her hands trembling.

Solomon glanced down at his fine suit, complete with brocade vest, in spite of the summer heat. "I figured it was best to do this properly," he answered, his thought process so like her own that it left her breathless.

And then they stood there, silent and awkward, merely smiling at each other, until they both broke into bashful laughter. Honoria wasn't sure she'd ever seen Solomon laugh before, and the sight made her heart ache. He was such a handsome man, and laughing like that made him all the more appealing. It would be so, so hard to leave him when the consumption finally took her, but until them, it would be like a glimpse into heaven to spend the rest of her days with him.

At last, he cleared his throat and straightened, tugging at the hem of his jacket. "Miss Honoria," he began.

"Yes?" Her heart fluttered.

It nearly stopped all together when Solomon dropped to one knee. She nearly begged him to get up to spare dirtying his tailored trousers, but by that point, she was beyond speech. He reached into his jacket pocket and took out a small, velvet box.

She knew why she was here. The proposal was happening at her insistence. She was the one who had begged him to marry her, to save the remainder of her life from misery. But when Solomon presented the box to her and opened it, revealing a simple, diamond ring, she brought her hands to her mouth in blissful shock as tears came to her eyes. As if proposing was his idea. As if he truly wanted to marry her instead of just feeling sorry for her.

"Miss Honoria," he repeated, his voice somehow thicker, deep with emotion. "I know that the circumstances surrounding us are far from ordinary, and I know that our time together will be short, but for what time we have, for what it's worth, will you make me the happiest man in Haskell by consenting to be my wife?"

*It isn't real*, a part of her cautioned. *He's just taking pity on you*. But in that moment, looking into the dark, mysterious, and tender depths of Solomon's eyes, Honoria could believe that this fine, noble man in front of her truly loved her. He was everything she'd ever wanted, and he was there for her.

"Yes," she whispered, her heart almost too full for her to form the word.

He burst into a smile that was far, far more genuine than she could have wished for, almost seeming surprised. He stood, taking the diamond ring out of its box, then slipping the box into his pocket. He reached for her hand and slid the ring on her finger.

"Whatever else," he said, holding her hand in both of his, "I promise that I will be as good of a husband to you as I know how to be. I can't say that everything will be as peaceful and easy for you as you'd like, but I'll do my best to make you happy and to—" He stopped suddenly, his expression pinching with emotion. When he went on, his voice was hoarse. "And to make your final days the best days of your life."

"That's all I ask for," she answered, blinking back tears but trying to smile all the same. "That's all I need." *You're all I need*, her heart answered as if it had longed to say those words for years.

Solomon nodded. For several long moments, he continued to hold her hand, staring into her eyes. Then, slowly but deliberately, he moved one hand to her waist and leaned down to kiss her. A sudden thrill of expectation coursed through her as he drew closer, his lips whispering over hers. The expectation burst into a fiery ball of longing as she tilted her head up and met his kiss with openness and acceptance. He was bigger than her in every way, his mouth wide and encompassing, and yet she trusted him with every part of her as his lips explored hers.

What started as a simple, closed-mouth kiss flared quickly into a full embrace. His hand slipped to the small of her back and tugged her closer. His lips parted hers, and she nearly sighed aloud as his tongue danced alongside hers. Shivers of heat and pulsing need poured through her, urging her to throw her arms around him, submit to him in every way a woman submitted to a man. She longed to lose what little of herself she had left in this brave, strong, kind man.

"Oh, it's so beautiful."

The sudden, joyful comment and the clapping that came with it nearly shocked Honoria out of her skin. She jumped back, wrenching free of Solomon's embrace and jerking to the side to find a trio of women standing in the street watching them. One had taken out a handkerchief and was dabbing her eyes while the other two continued to clap and beam.

"Ladies." Solomon nodded to them, his voice deep and his expression suddenly stiff and serious.

"That was simply the most beautiful thing I've ever seen," another of the women, this one with red hair, her bodice cut low, sighed.

Honoria blinked as recognition dawned. The three were Bonnie's girls. She remembered that the one with blond hair was Pearl, the one with red hair was Della, and the Spanish one was Domenica.

"I am truly, so happy for you," Domenica said in her thick accent.

"Thank you?" In truth, Honoria had no idea whether

to be pleased or terrified. The women were whores. They worked for Bonnie Horner. Honoria considered Bonnie a friend, but she was also her father's lover.

That last thought alarmed her as it sped through her head. She took a quick step toward the women. "Please don't say anything to Bonnie," she begged.

The three of them looked startled.

"Not say anything?" Pearl squeaked. "But Bonnie will be so happy for you."

Maybe she would be, but at the moment Honoria couldn't bear the thought of the one person in her daily life who didn't treat her terribly thinking badly about her for making such a sudden move. "I'll…I'll tell her in my own time," she said to the girls.

"It's just such a wonderful love story," Della sighed as the three of them nodded their agreement to keep things quiet. "Mr. Templesmith has always been such a gentleman to us all."

Honoria's brow shot up, and she turned to look at Solomon.

"Not in that way," he was quick to correct any misconceptions she had before they could truly form.

"He advised me about a bank account," Pearl said.

"And he explained to me that investing a portion of my earnings could help me to stop working this way three years sooner than I thought," Domenica added.

"It's the least I can do." Solomon smiled and nodded to them, his hands clasped behind his back. "I dislike seeing people in servitude of any kind," he added with a slightly ominous tone, glancing at Honoria.

Certainty that the decisions she'd made were good ones filled her along with certainty that Solomon was among the best of men.

"We'll just leave you to, you know." Della winked

and hooked her arms through Pearl's and Domenica's tugging them along.

"Congratulations again," Pearl called over her shoulder as the three of them rushed on, giggling.

Honoria watched them for a moment before letting out the breath she'd been holding and pressing a hand to her stomach. She had an uncomfortable feeling that they'd just experienced the most positive reaction to their engagement that they would receive.

"Are you all right?" Solomon came up behind her and rested his large hand on the small of her back.

Honoria nodded tightly, then turned to face him. She relaxed at his touch, smiled at the heartfelt concern in his eyes. "I'll have to tell Bonnie," she whispered, already dreading the conversation.

"I think so," Solomon agreed. He shifted his weight, a thoughtful look coming to his eyes. "I don't think she'll mind. She may not even be surprised."

Honoria's brow lifted at the thought. It was true, Bonnie had a keen eye for human nature. Honoria was still baffled as to why she had attached herself to Rex Bonneville, but she'd never been brave enough to ask. Perhaps now…

She shook her head at the thought. There were other, more pressing problems.

"I… I'd like to marry as soon as possible, if that's all right with you." She lowered her eyes just a bit at her brazenness.

"I agree." Solomon took her hands to reassure her. "I can speak to Rev. Pickering tomorrow morning to make arrangements."

Hope returning, she smiled up at him. "It isn't easy for me to get away from my father's ranch on my own, but Vivian's wedding on Monday will have everyone distracted." Monday was only two days away. "We could find a way to take advantage of the decorations in the church and the dress I've made for the occasion."

A wistful smile filled Solomon's expression, and he brushed a lock of her hair back behind her ear. "You never cease to amaze me, Honoria."

"Me?"

"Yes, you. You think so little of yourself, express so much concern for those who are not concerned for you."

Her lashes fluttered down. "I only have one family, difficult though they are."

"No you don't." He slid a hand under her chin to tilt her face up to him. "You have me now. I'm not much, but I'll be your family. It will be…" He stopped, his voice catching and his eyes filling with ragged tenderness. "It will be my name on your tombstone." He spoke the words quickly, as if he didn't want to say them but had stopped himself too late.

A warm, fluttery feeling filled Honoria's heart at the strangely romantic thought. Honoria Templesmith. Decades in the future, when everyone else was gone, any stranger finding her resting place would see that name, would never know the life she'd lived as a Bonneville.

"I'd like that," she whispered. "It's…it's how I want to be remembered."

"Then we'll make it happen," he said, bending down to kiss her lips gently. "Monday, we'll make it happen."

# Chapter Three

"Honoria!" Vivian's shrill shout echoed through the Bonneville house. "Honoria, where are you?"

"Get your lazy bones down here at once!" Melinda's echoing cry followed.

Honoria coughed hard enough to shake her poor lungs, but continued madly folding her clothes and stuffing them into the worn carpetbag she'd brought down from the attic after everyone had gone to sleep the night before. She worked as swiftly and silently as she could, cramming as much as would fit into the meager bag. If she couldn't fit it in the bag, she couldn't take it with her into her new life.

The sound of Vivian and Melinda's complaining voices continued downstairs, probably at the base of the stairs, but their words were indistinct. The tone was enough to light a fire under Honoria, though. She whipped back to her wardrobe and selected one more dress. The muted blue cotton was cool and comfortable and would suit her final days far better than any of the flashier, fancier gowns she owned. Not that she owned many. The fruits of her labor went to Vivian, Melinda, and sometimes Bebe, but rarely to herself.

"Honoria!" Vivian's shout was twice as irritated this time and came from halfway up the stairs. "Land sakes, what is your problem?"

Honoria gasped and folded the dress as quickly as she could as the thumping sound of Vivian marching upstairs came closer. She shoved the dress into the carpetbag, then snatched the open bag off of her bed, where she was loading it, and practically tossed it into the wardrobe.

She had just begun to shut the wardrobe doors when Vivian came crashing into her room, Melinda behind her.

"What is taking you so long?" The shrewish scowl on Vivian's otherwise pretty face was a stark contrast to her wedding dress. Honoria had labored for hours on the silk and lace confection. It had a full, stylish bustle, all the layers of flounces and ruffles that Vivian loved, and a stately, high collar which was currently fastened with their mother's cameo brooch. Honoria would have given anything to be able to take that brooch with her to Solomon's house.

Vivian must have seen the longing in Honoria's eyes. She clapped a hand over the brooch, narrowed her eyes, and hissed, "Don't you even think of it."

"Good Lord, Honoria," Melinda huffed, not noticing the interaction. She glanced around the room—which looked exactly as plain and tidy as it always did—and threw up her arms. "What can you possibly be doing up here? We're already running late."

Honoria opened her mouth to give some sort of explanation, but only ended up coughing.

"Ugh." Vivian scrunched up her face. "You're as bad as a leper. You should see Dr. Abernathy about that."

It was all Honoria could do to keep a straight face.

Before she could say anything, Vivian pushed on with, "I tore the hem at the back of my dress. Fix it."

"And then you can add a few more of those silk flowers to my bonnet," Melinda added.

Vivian rounded on her and demanded, "Which silk flowers?"

Melinda flushed. "Well, you're not going to use any more of them. It's a pity to have them go to waste after Papa sent all the way to Paris for them."

"Those are *my* silk flowers." Vivian raised her voice, fists clenched as she glared at Melinda. "No one will use them but *me*!"

Honoria kept her lips pressed tightly shut, at least until she burst into another coughing fit. She raised her hands to cover her mouth.

"I won't have you—" Vivian stopped dead in the middle of upbraiding Melinda and snapped to face Honoria. Or rather, to face her hand. Her eyes shot wide, then narrowed in bitter suspicion. "What in God's name is *that*?"

Sickly dread pooled in Honoria's stomach, and she jammed her hands behind her back. She'd forgotten to take Solomon's ring off. She'd been so careful to keep it in her pocket or hanging from a ribbon around her neck, close to her heart, in the two days since he'd given it to her, but she'd put it on that morning and forgotten to take it off.

"What's what?" she asked, voice trembling as she yanked the ring from her finger behind her back and tucked it into the folds of the small bustle at the back of her Sunday dress.

She could only pray that it stayed put as Vivian grabbed her arm and wrenched it forward. The gesture hurt, but Honoria would rather a moment of pain than discovery of her secret. She presented her other arm as well, holding out empty hands to her sisters.

"I saw something too," Melinda insisted. "She stole some of your jewelry, didn't she?"

"I didn't, I swear," Honoria said, truthfully.

Vivian narrowed her eyes. "You did, you little wench, and I'll prove it."

She swayed forward, tightening her grip on Honoria's wrist, but before she could say or do more, a call of, "Vivian, darling, the carriage is about to head into town," sounded from downstairs.

Footsteps followed, and Vivian yelped and whirled to face the door. "Don't come another step up those stairs, Rance Bonneville!"

The footsteps stopped. "Why not?" Rance asked in his Kentucky drawl.

"Because the groom does not see the bride before they meet at the altar, you dunce," she scolded him with a shout. "Don't you know anything?" Under her breath she muttered, "I'll never forgive Papa for making me marry him."

"I thought you wanted to get married," Melinda said. "You know, status and babies and all."

Vivian sent her sister a look as though she was an imbecile child. "You have to go through some very unpleasant things to get those babies," she growled, her face going red.

"Like what?" Melinda blinked, clueless.

Honoria blushed for her. Not that she knew much herself, but she knew the basic mechanics of making babies. How her sisters had dodged silly, whispered conversations in the schoolyard and contraband illustrations of technique that their father would have been outraged to know she'd seen was a mystery.

"Hurry up, Viv," Rance called from the stairs.

Vivian huffed and started toward the door. "You'll find out when your turn to marry comes," she told Melinda.

"Well, how did you find out?" Melinda demanded.

Vivian's expression went completely flat. "Bonnie told me."

Honoria hid her laughter with a cough. Not even the annals of Ancient Greek drama could come close to the animosity Vivian—and Melinda—felt for Bonnie, but if anyone knew the ins and outs of "relations," it was Bonnie. Honoria would have loved to be a fly on the wall of that conversation. Watching the two of them face each other down over breakfast that morning—Bonnie gracious and smiling, Vivian peevish and pouty—had been fine entertainment. Honoria would have loved to spend more time with Bonnie.

For many reasons, she realized as Vivian pushed Melinda into the hall to tell Rance to go away. Honoria was about to be married too, and though the time to discuss it hadn't come yet, she wanted to experience all of the happinesses of marriage. All of them. Those contraband pictures she'd seen in her school days had been on her mind a lot in the past few days with her form and Solomon's as the models.

"Vivian says you have to go on ahead to the church in the wagon." Melinda's voice carried up from the stairs as she gave her message to Rance. "You're not to see her before the wedding, so you have to go now. We'll come in the carriage behind you."

"Well, all right then. I can get Kirby to drive me," Rance replied.

As his footsteps retreated, Vivian grinned in triumph.

"If he continues with that sort of obedient behavior, this marriage will be a success." She indulged in a chuckle, then turned to Honoria. Her pleased expression turned sour. "You're so useless, sitting up here in your room coughing. Come downstairs and fix my dress at once."

Honoria obeyed, moving her engagement ring from her bustle to her pocket, if only because the sooner she fixed what Vivian needed fixing and sent her on her way, the sooner she could put her own plans in motion. Solomon would be driving out to the ranch at some point after he observed the rest of the Bonneville family entering town. His plan was to make sure as few people as possible were at the ranch when he arrived to pick her up, and then to whisk her away as fast as possible. Honoria's mind was so preoccupied with their plans that she barely heard the insults and slights that Vivian and Melinda hurled at her—or Bonnie attempting to curb them—or Bebe's whining and complaining that everyone was ignoring her.

The only part of Honoria and Solomon's plan that Honoria wasn't sure how to execute miraculously ended up taking care of itself.

"There isn't room for you in the carriage," Vivian snapped as she and Melinda, Bebe and Papa climbed into the borrowed conveyance. Bonnie stood to the side, waiting for the others to take their seats. The regular family carriage wasn't fancy enough for Vivian's wedding day, so Papa had borrowed the elaborate, open carriage of a friend of his in the Wyoming Stock Growers Association and had it shipped all the way from Cheyenne. "You'll have to walk into town."

"Yes, Honoria has to walk into town," Bebe added with a wicked grin, adjusting her voluminous skirts as she sat back in her secure place.

For once, Honoria had no desire to complain about

her treatment at all. She merely nodded and pretended to look down at her skirt and lament how dusty it would get.

"I'll go with her." Bonnie's offer had Honoria snapping her head up. She tried to hide her horror. "I'll drive her in my wagon."

"Oh, I couldn't ask you to do that," Honoria fumbled.

Vivian glared at her, but Melinda narrowed her eyes in calculation.

"It's not a problem at all." Bonnie smiled.

"Well whatever you do, we're going to be late," Vivian snapped. "Papa, let's go."

Rex Bonneville sighed at his daughter's command, then nodded to Bonnie. "I expect you to be prompt," he said, then gestured for his driver to go on.

Honoria's heart beat near her throat as the carriage lurched into motion, heading around the dusty drive in front of the house and then out along the lane toward the road to Haskell. She continued to watch it for far longer than she needed to, wishing there was some way to send Bonnie on her way as well.

"Now, would you like to tell me why you asked my girls not to tell me how you and Solomon Templesmith got engaged the other night?" Bonnie cut right to the chase.

Honoria flinched and winced as she slowly turned to face Bonnie. The regal woman had her arms crossed and was trying hard not to smile, but as much as her lips twitched and tightened, her bright blue eyes were alight.

"I…" Honoria had no idea at all how to answer her. She could only pray that her and Solomon's plans weren't about to be dashed to bits. "I…"

Bonnie brushed her nerves away with a flick of her hand. "No need to act like brimstone is going to rain down on you. I couldn't approve of your engagement more."

That was even more startling. Honoria stared off into the distance where the dust from her family's carriage was moving further away, then scanned the yard around the ranch to make sure there were no ranch hands nearby. But no, they had all been ordered to attend the wedding. The only person left on the ranch was Maria, and she already knew what was going on.

"You don't have to look like that." Bonnie loosened her stance and stepped closer to rub Honoria's arm. "I'm happy for you. I've seen the way the two of you steal looks at each other when you think no one is watching."

Honoria blinked wide. "We do?"

Now it was Bonnie's turn to look confused. "Of course you do. I've always assumed the two of you were courting in secret."

"How…" Honoria's mouth hung open for a second before she closed it and shook her head. "We haven't been."

Bonnie's perplexed frown deepened. "Then how did this all happen?"

"I…" Heavens, she'd turned into a ninny who couldn't even string words together. But how did you explain something as horrible and tragic as her fate? At last, Honoria sighed and motioned for Bonnie to follow her back to the house. As they reached the porch and climbed up toward the front door, she let it all spill out. "I'm dying."

Bonnie gasped and reached out a hand to stop her before they walked through the door. "Oh, my dear, no."

Honoria swallowed and faced her. "Yes." She took a deep breath. "I went to see Dr. Meyers about my cough. He examined me. He even ran a modern test." She shrugged. "I have consumption. Dr. Abernathy tells me I have less than a year left." Once again, tears filled her eyes at the thought. But no, she was tired of crying over her fate. All she wanted to do now was take what was left of her life into her own hands.

"Sweetheart, I'm sorry." Bonnie wrapped her in an embrace that would have been motherly if Bonnie herself weren't so young. Young but wise beyond her years. Like a big sister. A kind, considerate big sister, not like Vivian or Melinda.

As quickly as she'd hugged her, Bonnie rocked back and held her at arm's length. "Wait, Dr. Abernathy told you? I thought you said Dr. Meyers."

"Dr. Meyers performed the exam, then he was called away. He gave his files to Dr. Abernathy to follow up."

"Ah." Bonnie sighed, her shoulders lowering. Honoria continued into the house and upstairs to her bedroom. "So…how does Solomon figure into this tragic news?"

As she reached the top of the stairs, Honoria turned to her, mustering a smile. "I ran into him shortly after I found out. You're right about me having tender feelings for him." She blushed and continued into her room to collect her carpet bag. She lifted it back to the bed and added a few more personal items, including a small daguerreotype of her mother, before closing it and fastening the clasp. "I don't know what came over me, I just knew that I couldn't live the last days of my life the way I've lived all the rest of them."

Bonnie's stricken expression softened into teary understanding. "I don't blame you."

"So I asked Solomon to marry me," Honoria admitted bashfully. "I asked him to take me away from this life for what time I have left. He said yes." She reached into her pocket to retrieve her ring, putting it back on her finger. "He gave me this."

Bonnie took Honoria's hand, blinking back tears, and studied the ring. "This must be what Pearl was telling me about. Please forgive her for spilling the beans," she rushed to add. "She means well, Pearl does, but she's always been impulsive."

"As long as you don't try to stop me, I'm fine with you knowing."

"Stop you?" Bonnie laughed. "Honey, I'm encouraging you to run as fast as you can into Solomon Templesmith's arms."

Honoria's brow flew up. "Even though he's a negro?"

Bonnie scoffed and brushed the question away. "Trust me, sweetheart. In my line of work I've seen all men of all races. The only thing different about them is skin deep, and the color of that skin in no way determines how cruel or kind, how smart or stupid, how ambitious or how lazy they are."

Honoria's jaw dropped at the revolutionary statements.

Bonnie wasn't done. "There are far worse men in this town who you could hook your fate to, and I think Solomon will make the…" Her voice faltered for a second, but she cleared her throat and went on in a gentler tone. "I think Solomon will make the last days of your life beautiful ones."

"I hope so." Honoria lowered her eyes. But no, that didn't seem right. She raised them and met Bonnie's boldly. "I know so. I've dreamed of being married to him for years." It felt right and natural to confess to Bonnie. "He…he kissed me the other night, and it was glorious."

Bonnie's grin turned mischievous. "Glad to hear it. Are you planning to be fully married to him?"

Honoria nodded and blushed.

"Then let me give you a few words of advice." She hooked her arm in Honoria's and picked up the carpetbag for her. The two of them headed downstairs to the porch to wait for Solomon. In the time it took for him to arrive, Honoria learned far more than a few forbidden drawings could ever have taught her, and every bit of it filled her with delicious sensations of excitement and anticipation.

Solomon wasn't sure if he should be grateful or suspicious that it was so easy to make it out to the Bonneville ranch undetected. He'd sat on the porch of The Cattleman Hotel, sipping coffee with Theophilus Gunn, who knew full well what was going on. Whether they were his to tell or not, it was impossible to keep a secret from Gunn. As soon as Rex Bonneville and his daughters had driven past on their way to the church, Solomon hopped down, strode around the corner, and climbed into his waiting wagon. He'd passed a few wagons of people dressed for a wedding on his way out, but no one bothered to stop and ask him what he was doing.

The only hint of uncertainty he felt was as he drove up the drive to the Bonneville house and saw that Honoria wasn't alone on the porch. Bonnie Horner sat with her. He braced himself for the distinct possibility that Honoria had been talked out of her decision, or that she'd changed her mind on her own.

"Morning Miss Honoria, Miss Bonnie." He touched the brim of his hat as he pulled his wagon parallel to the porch. He shifted across the bench, then hopped down as Honoria and Bonnie stood. He made eye-contact with Honoria, attempting to figure out if her mood had changed. "Are you ready?"

To his surprise, Honoria turned to Bonnie with a beaming smile of thanks. Bonnie stepped forward and hugged her, then escorted her down the stairs to where Solomon waited.

"You take care of her now," Bonnie ordered him, dabbing at her eyes with her gloved hand. "Honoria is a very special woman."

An explosion of relief and agreement spread through Solomon's chest. "She is that." He reached for Honoria's hand.

Still smiling, looking paradoxically like the picture of health and happiness, Honoria took his offered hand and stepped closer. In spite of the fact that they were miles from the church, surrounded by nothing but empty ranchland, just the three of them, he felt the same pride and responsibility as if Honoria had been given to him at the altar.

"Oh, let me get Honoria's things for you." Bonnie turned and lifted her skirts to dash up the porch stairs.

Solomon shifted his focus to helping Honoria into his wagon. She seemed determined to climb up herself. Or perhaps she simply wasn't used to being helped in any way. As he closed his hands around her waist and lifted, she gasped. Was it his imagination or did he feel a tremor of excitement zing from her to him?

"Comfortable?" he asked as soon as she was settled.

Her cheeks were pink, her eyes bright with adventure. She nodded. He nodded in return. It was a wonderful thing to be able to communicate so much with someone without using a single word.

"Here you go." Bonnie returned with a small carpetbag.

Solomon frowned. "Is that everything?" Knowing the Bonneville family, he expected her to bring along three trunks at least. Then again, knowing the Bonneville family, he could have expected much less.

"I couldn't pack all of my dresses without arousing suspicion," Honoria said as he took the bag from Bonnie and handed it back up to him. "Maybe there will be a way to send for them once…once the truth is known."

Solomon shook his head, walking around the back of the wagon to climb up on his side. "I'll buy you all new dresses," he declared. "I've always thought that you deserved much finer fare than I've seen you walking around town in."

"I don't mind my clothes," Honoria said, but there was a hint of hesitation, a dash of enthusiasm in her voice.

Solomon answered it by winking at her. The joy that spread across Honoria's face was enough to make him feel like the tallest man in the world.

As he gathered up the leads to tap his horse into action, Honoria stopped him with an intake of breath. "Bonnie, would you like a ride to town?"

"You two lovebirds go along," Bonnie replied with a teasing grin. "I have my own wagon to drive into town."

"Thank you." Honoria waved to her as Solomon waited until their exchange was finished before driving. "Thank you for your help."

"Don't thank me yet," Bonnie said, her mirth fading. "You might need much more of my help once your father finds out about this."

The simple, truthful comment dampened all three of their moods. Solomon nodded to Bonnie, then urged his horse on. He and Honoria were both silent until they'd driven all the way off of the Bonneville property and onto the road heading into town.

"We can swing past my house first," Solomon said at last. "That way you can drop off your bag and get a sense of what lies ahead." Or change her mind if she wanted to.

She blinked at him. "You have a house?"

He couldn't help himself. He laughed. "Of course I do. Where did you think I lived?"

"At the bank."

He nodded in understanding. There was a small apartment in back of the bank. "That apartment belongs to my employee, Horace Greeley, now. I haven't lived there for five years. Don't you remember the commotion when I announced I was building a home on Schoolhouse Loop?"

She relaxed a little, the lines of her face softening as they fell into easy conversation. "I thought the fuss was that you were financing the building of several houses along a street that some people wanted to reserve for shops and businesses."

Solomon laughed. "'Some people' being your father?"

"Well, yes." She lowered her head to stare at her hands, folded on her lap. A moment later, she popped her head up. "You live in one of those houses?"

"I do." He nodded. "The one at the end of the circle that turns into Station Street."

A worried expression came over her. "That's so near the church."

Guessing her concerns, he said, "We'll loop around the back way to avoid anyone from your family who might be lingering outside spotting us together too soon."

She seemed satisfied with the answer, and he drove on, taking them exactly the way that would draw the least attention. On the one hand, it felt wrong, dishonest somehow, to be sneaking around with the woman he would be married to before the end of the day. On the other, he knew just what kind of opposition they could potentially run into if anyone so much as had a hint of what they had planned. He wasn't about to risk ruining Honoria's chance at a few months of happiness to soothe his own pride.

He was fortunate to have a side entrance to his property from the back, through an alley that ran between the saddler's shop and one of the warehouses Howard had recently built for goods coming in on the train. As he'd hoped, no one saw him as he drove his wagon into the small but serviceable stable at the back of his property. He was quick to help Honoria down, then just as quick to unhitch his horse, letting it go in the fenced-in back yard.

"I wish I could present the house to you through the front door," he said, taking her bag—which she'd industriously fetched for herself—and encouraging her to rest her hand in the crook of his other arm. "The architect did a magnificent job. It presents quite a picture from the front."

"I'm certain it's beautiful no matter how it's approached."

Solomon smiled. There was something so positive and bright about Honoria, in spite of the hardship she'd endured. It was as if she expected to be delighted with anything and everything that was not associated with her family.

Still, he felt self-conscious as he led her up the back porch and in through the kitchen door. The kitchen was spacious and equipped with as many modern conveniences as he could find out in the west. Howard had the foresight to design the town for the latest advances in modern plumbing—innovations that were usually only found in cities and prosperous towns back East—so Solomon's house came complete with indoor running water and washroom facilities. His furniture was well-made, even if there wasn't much of it. As he led Honoria from the kitchen to the dining room, then around to the front hall and stairs, her wide eyes took in everything. Solomon beamed with pride.

Right up until she said, "You don't have much in the way of decoration, do you?"

His proud smile faded. He looked around with new eyes, with feminine eyes. "I haven't gotten around to purchasing artwork," he admitted.

"Or curtains?" she asked, breaking away from him long enough to cross the hall and touch the simple, raw muslin he had hanging in his front windows for privacy.

"Or curtains," he admitted with a sheepish sigh.

She met that sigh with an encouraging smile, then walked past him and up the stairs to the second floor.

"Why, there's only one room up here that's furnished at all," she exclaimed, nearly laughing as she did.

"Yes, well." He followed her up, inviting her into his bedroom and setting her carpetbag on the bed. "I haven't had the time to order a second bedroom suite for you, but in the meantime, I can sleep on the sofa downstairs."

She blinked at him, the color draining from her face. "You mean, you don't want to…" She cleared her throat, and as she did, a dangerously sweet rush of desire swirled up his spine. "That is, I assumed we would share a room, as married people do."

Tender compassion, hope, and a far baser emotion that affected his body as strongly as his heart fired through him. "I thought perhaps you wouldn't want that."

"Oh, I do," she answered so quickly that parts of him leapt for joy. She lowered her eyes, looking demure, and causing blood to surge even faster to inconvenient parts of him. "That is, I thought I had made clear that I wanted to experience a real marriage in the time I have left, not just a close friendship or…or an occasional taste of passion." She lifted her eyes to meet his. "That involves both going to sleep together and waking up together, doesn't it?"

He didn't trust himself to speak without sounding

like a wolf on the prowl until he'd cleared his throat and swallowed. "It does." He prayed he wouldn't frighten her with the sudden intensity of his passion. Although, if he was honest with himself, it wasn't sudden. Male as he was, he'd entertained far more fantasies of the ways the two of them could be together in the last few years than was strictly proper. To know that he would now be able to live those fantasies was more than his body and heart could take.

He had a tremendous responsibility to her. He didn't want to let her down.

He knew he'd been silent too long, wondering how on earth he was going to perform as a husband to her without losing his head and frightening her—particularly considering how much bigger than her he was—when she bit her lip and took a hesitant step closer to him. He was almost tempted to step back in case she discovered just how much their conversation had aroused him.

"Solomon?" Her innocent, questioning tone and shy expression didn't help to tamp down the passionate feelings coursing through him. "Would you…"

"Yes?" His voice cracked, so he cleared his throat.

"Would you let me decorate your house?"

His heart stopped for a beat as the unexpected question hit him. He blinked. Then he burst into laughter. "Of course I'll let you decorate."

In a flash, the amorous spell that had been cast over him was broken. "It's well past time I had someone spruce this place up."

"Good." Honoria smiled. "I would like to accomplish something before I die."

Her statement was like a discordant note played in the middle of a beautiful sonata. The ache that had formed in his groin blasted to his chest, constricting it and his throat. He hated it, that reminder that their time together would be short.

"Whatever you want, my dear," he said as tenderly as he could. He stepped closer to her and took her hands, kissing each of them. His smile returned as he spotted his ring on her finger. "I will give you whatever you want."

Honoria wanted to stay in the tender comfort of Solomon's house, getting to know him better, but if she had any chance of actually pulling off her clandestine wedding, she needed to play along with her family's wishes for just one more hour. It was painful to tear herself away from Solomon's smile, to sneak out the back of his house, and to run along the busy street to the church. She encountered one bit of astounding luck when she met Bonnie walking in from the other direction.

"That's good timing." Bonnie grinned. She gave Honoria a reassuring squeeze of her hand before hurrying her along toward the church steps. "No one will suspect we didn't drive in together."

"Thank you."

Honoria would have said more, but before she had more than her toe in the door, Melinda grabbed her arm and yanked her the rest of the way inside.

"Where have you been?" she demanded, shaking Honoria before letting her go. The jostling sent Honoria into a round of coughing. "We don't have time for that now. The service is about to begin."

"Oh, this is wretched," Vivian groused from the other side of the door at the back of the church. Her face was red with anger, and her voluminous bouquet shook in her clenched hand.

"What is?" Honoria dashed to see if part of Vivian's dress had ripped or the hem had frayed again.

The dress was in perfect order, but Vivian whined, "I don't like any of these people."

A few of Haskell's townsfolk sitting in the back rows twisted to stare at her with offended looks.

"You invited them," Honoria whispered, sending an apologetic look to the offended guests.

"I wanted my wedding to be the biggest, most exciting, most unforgettable social event of the year," Vivian went on, her face shining with delight for a moment. Her eyes lost focus, as though she was imagining a wedding even grander than the one in front of her. Then she huffed out a breath and sagged. "There are too many undesirables in this town who I just can't stand."

As if on cue, Solomon stepped through the church door. He looked as fine and gallant as any man in town as he removed his hat and nodded respectfully to Vivian. His gaze danced past her to Honoria for the briefest moment, and his smile widened. Before anything could be given away, he walked on, finding a seat at the end of a row near the back.

"See what I mean," Vivian grumbled.

Melinda snorted. Bebe scoffed along with them, then tilted her head to the side and said, "I like his suit."

"His suit is neither here nor there." Rex stepped in, putting an end to the conversation. "We're all here. Let's get this wedding over with."

Honoria barely raised an eyebrow at Bonnie, who floated to Rex's side and took his arm with a hollow smile. She would never understand that pairing.

"I knew you were wearing a ring!"

Vivian's sudden gasp made Honoria's blood run cold. Once again, she'd forgotten to take Solomon's ring off before it was too late. Vivian stepped out of her place near their father's side and grabbed at Honoria's wrist.

"It looks like a diamond too." Her avaricious eyes narrowed. "I bet this is mine. I bet you stole this out of my jewelry box."

"It isn't," Honoria insisted, cursing herself for her carelessness yet again.

Vivian twisted Honoria's wrist and tried to clamp her hand around the ring to tug it off. "You don't have anything this nice, so it must be mine. Why, it's better than my engagement ring." She gasped and continued to attempt to yank the ring off Honoria's hand as she struggled to get away. "I bet you stole my ring and substituted this poor excuse for a diamond in its place."

It was a ridiculous idea, since they all knew full well that Vivian had worn her diamond as if it was part of the Crown Jewels since the second Rance had given it to her. But it was true that Honoria's diamond was bigger and of a higher quality.

"Give it," Vivian growled.

"Yeah, give it," Bebe egged her on from the side.

More than a few of the people sitting at the back of the church turned to see what the fuss was. The organist playing away at the front of the church even looked up to see what was going on.

"It's my ring," Bonnie said at last, stepping between Vivian and Honoria and separating them. She turned a stern frown on Vivian. "I said she could wear it today."

"Well, she's wearing it on the wrong finger," Melinda sniffed. "It's not like she's engaged or ever will be."

Honoria hid her reddening face with a sudden cough. It took every effort of will not to look to see whether Solomon was watching.

"This is ridiculous," Rex grumbled, grabbing Vivian's elbow and turning her back toward the front of the church. "Your groom is waiting. Go get married, already."

Sure enough, Rance was watching them from the front of the church with an expression that held the same sort of curiosity as if he was about to watch a bear-baiting. When Vivian was dragged around to face him, he broke into a dopey grin and waved at her. Vivian made a sound of disgust in her throat.

Rex nodded to the organist, who ended her song and began the wedding march.

"Oh, goody, it's my turn." Bebe pushed her way to the front of the Bonneville scrum and started down the aisle at a stately pace, dismissive smile on her upturned face. Honoria let out a breath and took the bouquet Bonnie offered her before moving into place.

Before she could start her march, Rex grabbed her arm and said, "I don't want to hear another sound out of you, missy, not even a cough."

Honoria swallowed. She sought Solomon out amongst the congregation. His expression was concerned, but he nodded subtly and smiled. She smiled back, and told her father, "Not a peep."

Rex let her go, and she began her march up the aisle. Rance stood waiting for Vivian with one of the Bonneville ranch hands as his best man. Truth be told, Rance looked as much like a ranch hand as anyone else, in spite of being their third cousin. He may have carried the Bonneville name, but he was about as ignorant and uncouth as they came. He certainly didn't hold a candle to Solomon.

That thought pushed Honoria forward and made her tense smile blossom into something genuine. She didn't have plans to march down the aisle for her own wedding. That ceremony was likely to be rushed. This was it. This was her wedding march. She took a deep breath, imagining that it was everything that it should have been.

By the time she made it to the front of the church, Melinda was already halfway down the aisle, looking as smug as Bebe had as she walked. The three of them lined up to one side. Bebe elbowed Honoria out of the way so that she could stand closer to the action, even though, as youngest, she'd walked down the aisle first. Honoria was more than happy to take a large step back, separating herself from the others. At last, Vivian started majestically down the aisle on their father's arm, looking every bit as cloying and overbearing as could be. The moment was all about her, so much so that when she reached the front of the aisle and bid a tearful—and fake—goodbye to their father, she didn't even look at Rance and certainly didn't take his hand when he offered it.

"Dearly beloved, we are gathered here today in the sight of God and these, our family and friends, to join this man and this woman in holy matrimony," Rev. Pickering began. He seemed a little uncomfortable, his back stiff and his smile forced, until he glanced around the congregation. It was as if he drew strength from them rather than the farce of a couple before him.

As he turned back to Vivian and Rance, his gaze met Honoria's and he smiled. A genuine smile. He knew what would come after this wedding. Solomon had informed him of the entire situation, and as far as Honoria knew, he approved heartily. His smile confirmed that. He took a breath, his shoulders relaxing, and went on.

"Marriage is a holy institution, ordained by God for the betterment of all mankind."

Honoria listened intently as Rev. Pickering went on, sharing his thoughts on the joys and benefits of marriage. She loved everything he had to say. At the same time, her heart ached. Every sacred duty of married couples—to love, honor, protect, and bring joy to one another—was something she wished she could do for far, far longer than the time she would have. She longed to give Solomon children, to give him a happy, loving family, but it wasn't to be. The best she could hope for was to leave him with happy memories.

Vivian's exasperated sigh brought her back to reality. Honoria could practically hear her sister tapping her foot impatiently under her dress. She almost groaned aloud when Rev. Pickering finished his sweet words and turned to the two of them for the vows.

"Rance Efraim Bonneville, do you take this woman, Vivian Eugenia Bonneville, to be your lawfully wedded wife?"

Rance's grin turned lopsided. "I do."

"And do you, Vivian Eugenia Bonneville, take this man, Rance Efraim Bonneville to—"

"I do," Vivian cut him off.

Rev. Pickering's jaw hung open for a minute, as if he would scold her or go on with the full words of the ceremony. Instead, he shrugged—barely noticeable—and said, "Then by the power vested in me, I now pronounce you husband and wife. You may kiss the bride."

Vivian made a sound as though that was the last thing she wanted to do, but Rance leapt at the permission. He swept his arms around Vivian and planted a noisy kiss on her lips. Vivian squealed and backed away, wiping her mouth with the back of her hand.

"You'd better not do that again," she warned him in a hiss.

"Sweetheart, I plan to kiss you up all day every day for the rest of our lives," Rance replied.

Vivian groaned, but the sound was mostly swallowed by the strains of the organ bursting into a final processional hymn. Vivian grabbed Rance's arm and swung him around to face the congregation. They all applauded and smiled, but Vivian faced them as though they were laughing at some joke. She yanked Rance forward and marched back down the aisle.

Melinda followed her, still wearing a regal air that said the show was really all about her. Bebe trailed her with the same sort of look.

Honoria thought about staying where she was, but her father caught her with a stern frown as she took a half-step back. She had no choice but to start forward, heading back down the aisle to the church's back door and stepping out into the sunlight.

"Don't you touch me!" Vivian yelled at Rance as they proceeded around the side of the church to where the white canvas tent that the town usually used for summer potlucks was set up. Vivian had wanted a much grander reception—something at the hotel, ideally—but she also wanted everyone in town to attend and fete her. So the church yard it was. Melinda and Bebe caught up to her and whisked her away from Rance and on to where the cake and the presents were set up.

Honoria swerved off in the other direction and dashed around the far side of the church. Rev. Pickering had a private entrance to his office there. The door was never locked, and she was able to slip back inside before anyone could notice she was gone. She tip-toed across the office and peeked from that door into the main part of the church, watching as the congregation filed out into the summer sun. Solomon stood but lingered to the side of the church, talking with Howard Haskell. To Honoria's surprise, Bonnie slipped back into the building once almost everyone else was gone.

As soon as she felt it was safe, Honoria opened the office door and made herself known. Bonnie—who was facing in her direction—saw her first.

"You'd better hurry," she said, marching down the aisle. "Rex is distracted and so are the girls, but who knows for how long."

A rush of giddy excitement swirled up from Honoria's gut, getting out in a giggle. Solomon reflected how she felt with a broad smile as he headed down the side aisle and took her hand.

"You know," Howard commented as he walked with them to the center of the chancel at the front of the aisle. "It dawns on me that the two of you make a very attractive couple."

"Thank you, Mr. Haskell." Honoria nodded.

"Psht!" He waved her comment away. "No one calls me 'Mr. Haskell.' It's Howard, now and always."

Whether it was Howard or Henry or Hammurabi, Honoria hardly noticed. She began to tremble slightly as Solomon hooked his arm through hers and tucked her close to his side.

"Are you doing all right?" he asked, his rich voice tender for her.

Honoria nodded in response, hugging his arm. This was it. Freedom was at her fingertips. She clutched the bouquet that she still held closer to her chest and her racing heart.

Rev. Pickering returned from the side of the room

with a small table, a fountain pen and a piece of parchment on top of it. "I've started having couples sign their marriage license before the ceremony," he informed them. "It comes in handy when they want to rush out and get settled in their new life." He handed the pen to Solomon and turned the parchment to face him and Honoria.

Another, deeper thrill rippled through Honoria's gut. This was it. This was real. She watched, holding her breath, as Solomon signed his name in a fine, neat hand. Jeremiah. His middle name was Jeremiah. She liked it. When he finished, he straightened and handed the pen to her.

"If you've changed your mind, I will understand." He spoke as though only the two of them were there, even though Rev. Pickering, Bonnie, and Howard looked on.

Honoria smiled with her whole heart and took the pen, their hands brushing. "This is what I want." Her voice cracked. She was so much more emotional than she expected she would be. "I…I think this is what I've wanted for a long time. I'm only sorry that I didn't say something sooner." Her final words dropped to a whispered hush.

With a look that was just full enough with regret to make Honoria's heart break, he lifted her left hand to his lips and kissed it. "I should have been brave enough to say something sooner myself."

"But we have each other now," Honoria rushed on, loathe to upset him any more than she knew she would in the months to come, as her health failed.

He nodded, holding her hand in both of his. "We do."

Honoria stayed right there, her hand and heart warming with the promise Solomon offered her. At last, she turned away and signed her name to the license. When she straightened, Bonnie was weeping outright, dabbing at her eyes with a handkerchief embroidered with the initials "HH." Howard was more than a little glassy-eyed himself as he watched the Honoria and Solomon.

"I think those are the sweetest vows I've ever heard, and the ceremony hasn't even started yet," he said.

"Then let's start," Rev. Pickering said with a wide smile. "Dearly beloved, we are gathered here today in the sight of God and these friends, to join these two in holy matrimony."

There was a marked difference in the simple, quiet service, as opposed to Vivian and Rance's ceremony less than half an hour before. Only five people were involved, but the emotion and sphere of love was a hundred times greater. Bonnie did her best not to sniffle as Rev. Pickering said a few words about love enduring beyond this life. Rev. Pickering himself spoke with a softer voice, leaned in toward Solomon and Honoria as he addressed them, and smiled with wistful grace throughout the entire brief ceremony. Honoria tried to soak it all in, to be in that moment for as long as possible, but like her poor life, it was over too fast.

"Do you, Solomon Jeremiah Templesmith, take this woman, Honoria Aurora Bonneville, to be your lawfully wedded wife, to have and to hold in sickness and in health, to love, honor, and cherish, until death do you part?"

"I do," Solomon answered with a tremor in his voice that both lifted and broke Honoria's heart. He slipped a gold ring on her finger to sit beside the diamond one, and Honoria's tears began to flow. She hadn't expected a wedding ring at all.

"And do you, Honoria Aurora Bonneville, take this man, Solomon Jeremiah Templesmith, to be your lawfully wedded husband, to love, honor, and obey in sickness and in health, until death do you part?"

"I do," she managed to squeeze out. "And even after that." She only wished she had a ring to give him as well.

Bonnie swallowed a moan, and even Howard cleared his throat to cover his emotion. Tears painted two hot trails down Honoria's face at the depth of affection in Solomon's eyes. He was so kind, so understanding, that she could almost believe he loved her as genuinely as if they'd enjoyed a long courtship and engagement.

"Then by the power vested in me," Rev. Pickering went on, "I now pronounce you husband and wife. What God has joined together, let no man put asunder." He leaned in and followed with, "You may kiss your bride."

Bonnie rushed up and took Honoria's bouquet, and as soon as her hands were free, Honoria reached for Solomon's. Solomon went beyond just holding her hands, though. He circled his arms around her waist and pulled her into a tender embrace. As gently as a cloud kissing the meadow, he covered her lips with his and sealed their union with a kiss. Honoria closed her eyes, opening herself to him, wishing this moment could last forever, that it wasn't the beginning of the end.

Solomon must have felt the urgency and torment of her heart. He tightened his arms around her and kissed her more deeply. What began as a touching of hearts deepened to something that whispered of so much more. Honoria reveled in it, curling her fingertips into the strong muscles of his back and willing him to take her away to a place where there was no sickness, no cruelty, and no prejudice. That was all the heaven she needed.

She was still soaring on the wings of happiness, wrapped in Solomon's arms, when the sharp shout of,

"What is the meaning of this?" crashed through the beauty of the moment from the back of the church.

They all turned to find Rex Bonneville standing in the church doorway, glaring as though he was ready to commit murder.

# *Chapter Five*

Solomon snapped to full alertness the moment Rex barked his question. His muscles tensed, ready to fight or take Honoria and run if he had to. The last time he'd felt such a hard urgency to act was when Martin Postern, his master's son, had whisked him off in the middle of the night to make a run for the North. As Martin had protected him then, so Solomon turned to shield Honoria from her father now.

"This is a private marriage ceremony, sir," he said with as much power and courtesy as he could manage. Always take the high road.

"*Marriage* ceremony?" Rex's eyes flared with fury.

Two townspeople had poked their heads into the church behind him. At Solomon's declaration, they gasped and scurried back out into the afternoon sunshine. No doubt within minutes, all of Haskell would know that Solomon Templesmith and Honoria Bonneville had eloped.

Rex must have understood every bit of the implication. Clenching his fists at his sides, he marched up the aisle to confront them. Honoria gasped, and Solomon could feel her faint trembling as she leaned into his back. He reached around and grasped her hand for comfort.

"In no way have I given anything even *close* to permission for a daughter of mine to marry the likes of *you*," Rex snarled as he came to within a few feet of Solomon. Howard stepped up to stand by Solomon's side, and even Bonnie reached a cautious hand toward Rex. Rex beat it away.

"I don't need your permission to marry, Papa." Honoria stepped out from behind Solomon's back and faced her father. Her voice wavered, and she looked as though she might shrink away if Rex raised his hand, but a burst of pride filled Solomon all the same. Even standing up to the man this much must have taken all the courage she had.

"I forbid this marriage to take place," Rex snapped.

"It's already taken place." Rev. Pickering joined the line of defense, coming down to stand on Solomon's other side.

"Then undo it," Rex glowered, face turning redder by the second.

"I can't." Rev. Pickering shrugged. "Moreover, I won't. This marriage was entered into with the full consent of both parties."

"It was not entered into with my consent!" Rex shouted.

"Excuse me, sir, but these two young people are not so young that they need your permission to wed," Howard bellowed right back at him.

Rex snapped to glare at Howard, so angry that a fine sweat beaded on his brow. "I will not allow any of my daughters of whatever age to marry a n—!"

Honoria gasped. Bonnie clutched a hand to her

stomach, seething with offense. Howard and Rev. Pickering both began to protest, but Solomon brushed the comment off as the desperate words of a man who knew he'd already lost his argument.

"I have pledged my troth to Honoria," he said, steady and resonant, refusing to refer to his new wife as Rex's daughter. "She has accepted my hand gladly and given me her own in the sight of God. There is nothing you can do about it, no matter who you think you are or who you believe me to be."

"Why, you uppity dog!" Rex raised a hand as if he would strike, but both Howard and Rev. Pickering leapt to intervene.

They didn't need to. Rex would never get close enough to strike him. Solomon was faster and stronger than him, and though he'd longed to teach the man a lesson he sorely needed, Solomon wasn't violent by nature. He continued to simply stand his ground, shielding Honoria as much as she needed to be shielded, and holding her hand.

"This marriage will stand," he said.

Rex used his raised hand to wipe the sweat from his face. His eyes focused on Honoria when he was done. "I demand you leave this man and come home at once!"

Solomon twitched to speak for her, but stayed silent to allow Honoria to say, "No, Papa. I won't."

"Honoria!"

She shook her head. "I'm a married woman now." Her voice was small but clear. "You don't own me."

The words stung that deep place in Solomon that knew exactly how it felt to be owned and exactly what it was to be free. He squeezed Honoria's hand tighter.

"You cannot do this," Rex continued to rail. "This marriage isn't legal without my consent."

"I'm twenty-five years old, Papa," Honoria said. "I have the right to make my own decisions."

"Not this one," Rex insisted.

"Rex, let it go," Bonnie spoke softly from the side.

Rex rounded on her, his fury redoubled. "And you! What part have you played in this farce, you interfering cat? My daughter is not one of your whores to be pimped out as you see fit."

"Now see here," Howard interjected.

Solomon bubbled with rage, ready to defend Bonnie as well if he had to, but Bonnie barely blinked.

"You've been involved in this all along, haven't you?" Rex blasted on, stepping closer to tower over Bonnie. Still, Bonnie barely flinched as she stared him down. "You encouraged me to find a husband for Vivian, and now you're complicit in this criminal activity. I can see right through you, missy. You're attempting to get rid of my daughters so you can sink your greedy little fingers deeper into my pockets."

"I can assure you that is not my intention," Bonnie replied, so calm that it had to be a mask. "My concern is for your daughters' happiness."

"Like hell it is," Rex bellowed. He raised a finger, pointing it at Bonnie, then said in an ominous voice, "I'll deal with you later."

Again, the urge to do whatever it took to protect Bonnie pushed through Solomon, but Rex didn't give him time to act. He whipped back to face Solomon and Honoria.

"I'm giving you one last chance to undo this travesty," he said in cold, warning tones.

"No," Honoria answered. Her answer was so simple that it sucked the very air out of the room.

Rex bristled in fury and turned to Solomon, murder in his eyes.

"No." Solomon echoed his wife. "I made a promise to Honoria, and I intend to honor it."

Silence crackled through the church. No one dared to move or breath.

At last, Rex bared his teeth in what could have been a wicked smile or a snarl. "You will regret this," he hissed. "I will hound your every waking moment and put every ounce of my power and influence to work bringing you down."

"You can try." Solomon met him with stoic calm.

Rex narrowed his eyes further. "If I can't end this marriage where it started, I can end it in other ways." His meaning was as clear as if he had laid out detailed plans for murder. "You'd do well to get your affairs in order."

Howard had only just opened his mouth to object, and no one else had had a chance to move, when Vivian burst in at the back of the church and shrieked, "My wedding is ruined!"

Strangely, the dark tension that had wrapped itself around the group at the front of the church snapped like a spring breaking loose from a clock. The sudden shift almost had Solomon laughing.

Vivian trounced up the aisle, her bouquet—looking a little worse for wear—still in one hand. Her face was twisted in an expression of peevishness.

"Rance keeps drinking whiskey instead of wine, only a few people have come up to tell me how beautiful I am, and now the only thing anyone is talking about is that *she* got married too?" Vivian reached the front of the aisle with her last complaint and pointed her bouquet at Honoria. "It can't possibly be true."

"It is true." Honoria stood straighter and inched forward, still holding Solomon's hand. "Solomon and I were married."

"No," Vivian yelped, not in protest, but as if she'd been told a ridiculous lie. "No, you weren't. You can't marry him, it's illegal."

"It is not illegal in my town," Howard answered, full of bombast, probably glad that he could finally say something to help the situation.

"Well you can't," Vivian went on in a grinding voice. "This is *my* wedding day, and I won't have you ruining it."

"Your sister hasn't ruined anything," Solomon said. "The reception out there is still for you. The cake and the gifts and the band is all yours."

"But everyone is talking about her," Vivian protested. "They're supposed to be talking about me!"

Solomon opened his mouth to reason with her, but Honoria squeezed his hand and shook her head. He closed his mouth. She had far more experience dealing with her sister than he did.

"We'll leave," Honoria said. "I can't stop people talking, but I won't stay around and detract from your party."

Vivian's face pinched as though she couldn't figure out whether that was a good thing or a useless one. "Fine," she huffed at last. "Go on. Get out of here. If you really did marry this...man—" She curled her lip as though she'd wanted to call him something else. "—then I don't ever want to see you again."

Solomon wondered if that would hurt or delight Honoria beyond telling.

Honoria nodded. "I wish you every happiness in your new life," she said, quietly but sweetly. She turned to her father. "I'm sorry to have disappointed you, Papa, but this was something I had to do."

"It was not—" Rex stopped cold when Solomon shot a silencing look his way. He bristled, rubbed a hand over his face, then seethed, "Go!"

With a quick sideways look to Solomon, Honoria pushed forward, silently leading him down the church's aisle and out the door.

Almost the entire town of Haskell was celebrating Vivian and Rance's wedding, and in spite of the rumors that were quick to spread through the revelers, Honoria and Solomon were able to sneak away without much notice. A few of their friends spotted them and ran to offer congratulations, but Solomon urged them to return to the party, saying there would be time for explanations later.

Honoria was grateful for his intervention. Her head was spinning after the encounter with her father. She could hardly believe that she had said the things she had. But from the moment her father had demanded she undo the one thing that had given her joy and confidence in her life, she knew that in that moment, her death was staring her in the face. She could either give in to it and die right there, simply fading away for the next few months, or live to the fullest while she could.

She chose life.

"Well, here we are," Solomon said as the two of them stepped through the front door of his house—their house.

Relief like nothing Honoria had ever felt filled her. She sighed and smiled. "Here we are."

Solomon shifted to study her. The expression he wore was just a little bit confused. To an extent, she understood his confusion.

"The worst is over," she explained with a shrug as

her happiness doubled and doubled again. "The rest of my life starts now."

His confusion resolved into a smile tinged with sadness. He turned toward her fully and took her hands. "And what would you like to do to start off the rest of your life, Mrs. Templesmith?"

A thousand ideas swirled in her mind. How strange to be able to choose what to do with her own time. Usually she spent her days running to complete one demand or another. She tilted her head to the side and pursed her lips in thought.

"I'd like to cook," she said at last.

"Cook?" Solomon's smile widened, and he laughed. "Cook what?"

"Anything." Honoria laughed along with him. "I was never allowed to cook at home. Papa always insisted we had a servant for that, and Vivian and Melinda were certain I'd burn the house down if I tried. But I managed to sneak down to the kitchen a time or two to help Maria."

Solomon's eyes danced with mirth. He shifted to settle her hand in the crook of his arm, then walked her down the hall toward his kitchen—their kitchen. "So what would you like to cook?"

It was dizzying to have so many choices in front of her. "Well, it's past lunchtime but not quite suppertime yet."

"We could get supper started," Solomon suggested. "Honestly, my cooking skills aren't the best, and between the two of us it might actually take that long to prepare anything."

"Good point." She giggled, mystified by how easy it was. "So what do you have in your pantry?"

As it turned out, Solomon had a lot of odds and ends in his pantry, but not a lot that made sense. There were sacks of beans and lentils, a large bag of potatoes, and a rasher of bacon. He had a few bunches of carrots and some turnips, plenty of flour and sugar and other baking supplies, but other than the bacon, no meat.

"I'd run out and buy you a chicken if I didn't think Mr. Kline had closed his store to attend the wedding," Solomon said as they lined the rest of the ingredients out on the kitchen table to see what could be done.

"Hmm." Honoria arched a brow. "I'm not sure we should start with something as complicated as chicken anyhow."

Solomon laughed. There was such a resonant and genuine sound to his laughter. Right then and there, she determined that she would make him laugh as much as possible so that she could wrap herself in the sound and take it with her to the grave.

"Do you have any books on cookery?" she asked, returning to the issue at hand.

"Plenty. I have plenty of books about every topic you could imagine."

Honoria gasped. "Truly?"

"Of course."

"I can't wait to read them all." She clapped her hands to her heart as if she needed to trap the joy she felt right where it was.

Again, a hint of sadness was betrayed in the twist of Solomon's mouth, the spark of his eyes. It wouldn't do to dwell on how quickly things would come to an end between them. Right now, all Honoria wanted was to imagine that their life together would go on forever.

Solomon fetched the cookbook while she laid out the rest of the ingredients from the pantry. Once that was done, the two of them stood side-by-side, flipping through the pages to see what their possibilities for supper were.

"We could actually attempt bacon pies," he said after they'd gone back and forth between a few recipes that called for few ingredients.

"Sounds delicious," Honoria hummed.

"Let's do it, then."

Bacon pie turned out not to be as simple as Honoria expected, but every minute of the challenge of mixing out pastry dough, chopping vegetables and bacon, and whipping up a broth to fill the pies was pure bliss. After a lifetime of working at odds with her sisters, it was the easiest thing in the world to work with Solomon.

"Two cups of flour?" he asked as he measured.

"Two and a half," she corrected.

He didn't scold her, he didn't blame her for being stupid, he just nodded and poured the correct amount of flour into the bowl.

As the afternoon and their work progressed, they didn't chat much. Most of their topics of conversation revolved around what they were doing. There was something so freeing about that, about focusing on the moment without worrying about the past or the future. The only time that they sat still and just talked was when the pies were baking, but even then, they spoke of the kinds of decorations that the house needed, what they could buy in town, and what needed to be ordered.

It was the most pleasant afternoon Honoria had ever spent, and by the time they were sitting across the small kitchen table from each other, eating their pies with a small glass of wine each, Honoria found an appetite she never knew she had.

"Between you and me, I think this was the most delightful meal of my life," she sighed happily, pushing her plate back when she was done.

"You know, I think you're right." Solomon echoed

her gesture and her posture, stretching his arm over the back of his chair. He looked every bit the lion stretching in his lair after a satisfying meal. "I bet we enjoyed it far more than any of the guests at your sister's fancy reception."

"Undoubtedly," Honoria laughed. "I imagine Vivian spent the rest of the party going around demanding that her guests talk about her and nothing but her."

Solomon laughed and shook his head. "I'd like to deny that someone could be that vain, but I've observed too much of your sister."

"I feel sorry for her, really," Honoria went on. "The only reason she talks about herself is because she isn't confident with any other topic."

Solomon's brow shot up. "That's mighty generous of you, all things considered."

Honoria sighed. "I don't hate my sisters. It's not their fault they've been indulged to the point where they don't know how decent folk should act."

Solomon shook his head. "Yep. Far, far too generous of you." His smile warmed. "Where did you learn to be so kind-hearted?"

"From my mother," she answered without even having to think about it. "She was the kindest soul you could imagine, and I made a promise to her that I would be honorable as well."

The affection in Solomon's expression not only made Honoria feel as though she'd said the right thing, it fired her blood, making her wonder what came next. The sun was already setting, and it would be night soon, her wedding night.

"We should clean up," she said, rising and taking her plates to the sink. She could feel her cheeks burning with expectation. Would she have to ask Solomon to take her to bed or would it just naturally happen? Bonnie had explained many things, but not how it all got started.

"I still have one question," Solomon said as he came to join her by the sink, drying dishes as she washed them.

"Oh?"

A wry grin spread across his face. "How did a woman who sounds as wonderful as your mother end up married to Rex Bonneville?"

Honoria laughed aloud at the question, impertinent though it was. "Papa wasn't always the way he is now. Mama used to tell me that he was a dashing, bold figure in his younger days. Very romantic. She fell for him like a prince in a story." Like she had fallen for Solomon. She swallowed the thought, turning her blushing face away from him, and went on. "Papa only really became cold and distant and argumentative after I came along and still wasn't a son, or so I'm told. When Mama finally did produce a son but died in the process, little Rex with her, he closed off entirely."

"I'm sorry, I didn't know." Solomon finished drying the last plate and turned to rest his backside against the counter. "I suppose it's true that no one is born disagreeable."

"Except Vivian and Melinda," Honoria tried to joke.

She wasn't sure Solomon heard her. She wasn't sure whether she'd heard herself. Solomon was studying her with a look that was equal parts puzzlement and temptation. She had so little experience with men, but instinct told her the flash of heat in his eyes was a prelude to exactly what she wanted.

"Solomon, I want to go to bed with you," she blurted before she lost her nerve. Instantly, her hands and feet went numb and her face flared hot. She could hardly bear to watch him as his expression registered first shock, and then something warm and sweet that she couldn't put a name to.

"Is that really what you want?" he asked.

She nodded, unable to form words.

Solomon smiled and pushed away from the counter to face her. "I wasn't sure if you'd really thought it through when you said so before." He took her shaking hands. "I'm happy to simply be your shelter and your friend until…" He let his words drift away, took a breath, and went on with, "I don't want you to feel as though…intimacy is something you owe me."

"Oh no," she spoke up, bubbling with awkward excitement. "I…that is, I had hoped from the first, when I asked for your help, that you would care to share *all* of life's experiences with me."

His smile grew, but he still looked baffled.

"I'm not afraid," she went on, feeling he wasn't quite convinced. "Bonnie explained things to me, and it sounds delightful, actually."

He laughed aloud. The sound sent shivers through her. "Well, if Bonnie explained things, I'm not so sure I can live up to them."

Honoria blinked. "No?" Oh dear. Was she out of her depth again?

Solomon slid closer to her, letting go of her hands to slip his arms around her in an embrace. "But I'm willing to try."

Relief flowed through her as he bent down to kiss her, his lips brushing, then enveloping hers. A moment later, that relief ignited into something just as taut as her anxiety, but infinitely more enjoyable. She let her strength give way to his, relaxing into his arms and arching her body into his.

He must have liked that simple show of acceptance.

His kiss deepened, and she could feel the tension pulsing through him. She parted her lips to allow his tongue to explore, and was even bold enough to tease her way through the kiss with him. He lowered a hand to cup her backside, and the blissful new sensations scattered throughout her body began to center and ache in her core.

"This will be far more comfortable if we do it in bed instead of in the kitchen," he whispered, notes of both humor and passion in his voice.

"Yes, of course," she breathed. At the same time, she could hardly let go of him long enough to let him walk her out of the kitchen, down the hall, and up to his bedroom.

The sight of his large bed—decorated with a simple, faded quilt—had Honoria's heart beating faster than she was sure was good for her. She checked herself to determine if any of her excitement was from fear. Perhaps the tiniest bit, but that fear flew away as soon as Solomon took her in his arms again for another kiss. Kissing him was pure heaven. His arms felt so right around her, and his mouth ravishing hers was beyond any joy she could have dreamed of.

"We have to take off our clothes," she panted restlessly, feeling like a fool for speaking something so obvious aloud.

"Yes, we do," Solomon answered with a patient smile. "Would you like me to undress you?"

The very idea sent shivers down Honoria's spine. Was that what you were supposed to do? Did Solomon know his way around all of the buttons and hooks and fastenings of her clothes?

"Um, it might be faster if we undress ourselves," she mumbled.

His smile grew even wider, and he nodded. "All right, if that's what you want."

Was it? Yes. She needed to be practical here. But as she stepped to the side and reached up to undo the hidden buttons down the front of her bodice, her eyes stayed glued to Solomon. He'd taken off his suit jacket hours ago, when they were cooking, but he'd left his vest on. He unbuttoned that now, peeling it off to reveal a crisp, white cotton shirt. Her seamstress's eyes was impressed by how well-made the shirt was. Her woman's eyes only wanted to drink in the sight of his firmly muscled torso and intriguing mahogany-brown skin as he pulled the shirt up over his head.

It struck her that she knew nothing about her new husband's form. She'd seen plenty of the ranch hands who worked for her father with their shirts off, but Solomon's body had always been a mystery wrapped in fine, gentleman's clothes. She was surprised by the sight of his flat abdomen, his well-shaped, strong arms, and firm chest with just a sprinkling of hair. He turned around to set his shirt and vest aside, and a sharp bolt of fear that she would see old welts from his younger days as a slave gripped her. But his back was as smooth and well-muscled as any man's. She breathed a sigh of relief.

That relief lasted until he undid the fastenings of his trousers and pushed them down over his hips. Honoria froze at the sight of his bare, powerful backside and thick thighs. She drank in the sight of him as he tugged his shoes off and stepped out of his pants. Every movement he made was like perfect, male poetry. It still didn't prepare her for when he turned to face her.

Her body was already frozen, but now her heart stopped in her chest at the sight of his full glory. She'd only ever seen pictures of the male anatomy, and none of them did  the real thing  a  lick of justice.  Or maybe it was just Solomon. His staff hung somewhere between relaxed and majestic against the backdrop of narrow hips and other, mysterious parts of his body. It seemed to be increasing even as she stared at him…perhaps *because* she stared at him. A voice in her whispered that polite women should be startled or shrink from something so quintessentially masculine, but Honoria found herself wanting to touch and explore and learn.

"I thought the object here was that we *both* undress."

Honoria didn't realize that she was staring—or that she hadn't even begun to remove her own clothes—until Solomon's teasing comment caught her off-guard. "Oh, dear." She dragged her eyes away from the sight of him and worked the buttons of her bodice with frantically shaking fingers.

It didn't help when Solomon stepped closer to her, like a panther stalking his pray. Heavens, her eyes wanted to focus on one thing and one thing only. Her fingers were completely useless.

"Let me," Solomon whispered as he came close. The heat and scent of him swirled around her.

Honoria could only let out a shaky breath and lower her arms. He reached up and finished with the buttons she had started to undo. With soft movements, he pushed her bodice back from her shoulders and set it on the chair behind her. To do so, he had to lean even closer to her, to the point where his body brushed against hers.

She sucked in a breath and lifted her hands to rest on his hips. The muscle, bone, and sinew that met her exploration brought the ache in her core to a fevered pitch. She tilted her head up, hoping to steal a kiss. Instead, he reached his arms around her to unhook the fastenings at the back of her skirt. His breathing had grown harder somehow, more ragged. She slid her hands around his hips to test whether the muscle of his backside was as powerful as she thought, and was rewarded by not only confirmation of the fact, but by those muscles flexing.

Solomon made a delicious, low sound in his throat. Her skirt sagged loose. He tried to push it down, but it caught on the layers of her underthings.

"Petticoat," she whispered.

He nodded once, then sent his hands exploring in the folds of her skirt for the ties that would free her. As he did, she stroked her hands up over his hips and around to the front. He sucked in a breath of expectation. She wasn't sure she dared to go any further, but the desire pumping through her was relentless.

At last, as he found and tugged the string of her petticoats, causing the whole mass of her skirts to sink heavily down her hips, she brought her hands around to explore him. They both gasped for breath as her hands closed around his thickening staff. It had somehow expanded in the last few minutes and now surged upward, standing tall. That was perfect, as far as she was concerned. It meant she could stroke him the way she wanted to, learning the new shape in all its intricacies. His tip had grown more flared as the rest of him stood stiff, the very top shining with hints of moisture.

"Honoria," he sighed, the sound making her whole body quiver, as he pushed her skirts down.

This time they dropped easily to the floor. Without waiting, he lifted her right out of the puddle of fabric and shifted to lay her across his bed. The shift in gravity left her gasping and hungry for more.

He paused long enough to tug her shoes off, then joined her on the bed, positioning himself over top of her.

"You're the most beautiful thing I've ever seen," he whispered. The rumble of desire in his voice did things to her that she was certain were scandalous.

"So are you," she panted in return, reaching for him.

He caught one of her hands and brought it to his lips for a kiss, then bent down to bring that kiss to her lips. Being kissed standing up and fully clothed was delightful. Being kissed while lying on her back, wearing nothing but her underthings, the man above her wearing nothing at all, was an entirely different level of wonderful. She could feel the pull of instinct urging her to meld herself with him. More than anything, she wanted to spread her legs open and embrace Solomon with her full body.

"Solomon," she urged him, not knowing how else to tell him what she wanted.

He replied with a deep hum that only made the longing worse. His hands shifted to the hooks of her corset, and blessedly, he made quick work of it. She arched so he could tug it out from under her and throw it aside. Then he grabbed the hem of her chemise and lifted it over her head with quick, hungry movements.

It felt glorious to be exposed to him, more so when he shamelessly raked his hands up from her stomach to cup her breasts. She should have been shocked to have him fondle her that way, his thumbs rubbing across her taut nipples, his touch possessive, but, in fact, she wanted more. Without words to say as much, all she could do was mewl with pleasure.

She got her 'more' when he adjusted his stance over her so that he could bring his mouth down to suckle her. The sudden sensation of her breast being enveloped in sweet, liquid heat as he laved his tongue across her nipple had her crying out for release. She dug her fingernails into his shoulders, wondering how she was going to maintain her sanity.

"I can't," he groaned at last, shifting again to bring his eyes level with hers. For one horrified moment, Honoria could only gape at him. "I can't draw this out," he went on, breathing heavily. "I want so much to pleasure you until you're giddy, but I'm about to burst."

She didn't entirely understand what he was saying, but it excited her beyond reason all the same.

"We'll have so much more time," he promised, his hands venturing down to find the drawstring of her drawers, the last piece in the puzzle of undressing. "I promise you, I'll make it all up to you over and over again."

The only thing she could manage to say was, "Yes," as he loosened her drawers and drew them down her legs. That final gesture left her completely naked and on fire. She was already primed to part her legs as he raked his hands up along her calves and thighs, drinking in the sight of her the same way she'd feasted on the sight of him. And she loved every moment of his scrutiny.

He had one more surprise in store for her. Tugging off her drawers had shifted him lower, and as his hands traced their way up over her thighs, his mouth followed. He kissed first the inside of one thigh, then the other, then back again, bringing his mouth higher as he nudged her legs further apart. She was beyond breathless by the time he reached the top of her thighs with both his hands and mouth. She'd opened her hips as far as they could go, her knees falling to the side. The only warning she had of what he was about to do came as his fingers gently parted her most intimate folds. Then he brought his mouth down on the most sensitive part of her.

The result was as powerful as thunder. The moment his tongue grazed the bulb of pleasure that had been growing increasingly sensitive, she nearly shouted with pleasure. One tiny spot, and it had her aflame with need. That need was met in spectacular fashion as he licked and swirled and sucked. In mere moments, her body exploded with light and hunger, the vibrations reaching so deep that she thought she would die right that moment. It would have been worth it.

He surprised her again by adjusting on top of her as she was still lost in the throes of orgasm, then crashing into her. Bonnie had warned of a moment of pain, but if there was one, she was too far gone with ecstasy to feel it. The sensation of being filled and stretched and possessed was beyond anything she could comprehend and so good that she wanted to weep.

And it still didn't stop there. As her own tremors slowed, she could feel Solomon's thrusts more fully. They were magnificent, pure, and carnal. He had already lost himself in the passion between them and thrust with wild abandon. Again, a tiny voice whispered that she should probably be frightened of his fierce intensity, but she absolutely adored every hard, pounding thrust. She adored the uncontrolled sounds of pleasure he made as he took her. The bed banged hard against the wall in time to his thrusts, and creaked so loudly she thought it might break, and she loved every minute of it. She clamped her arms around him, digging her nails into his back, and came close to laughing with the abandonment of it all.

At last, Solomon tensed and cried out. The sound was so perfect that she cried out with him, and when he collapsed, utterly spent, on top of her, she wrapped her arms and legs around him tightly. In a moment, the dynamic between them had shifted, and now she was the one who needed to provide comfort and affection and a safe place to land. He'd given all of himself to her—whether he'd intended to or not—and she held that close to her heart like a precious gem. This man who lay exhausted in her arms had given her so much, but now she understood that she had much to give him in return.

# Chapter Six

Honoria stretched and smiled with morning's first light. Her first dawn as a wife. She drew in a deep breath and curled against Solomon's side. Her husband was still fast asleep, and as far as she was concerned, he deserved every moment of rest he could find. They'd only slept intermittently through the night anyhow, napping off and on between long, delicious bouts of love-making. That first, explosive time had been a revelation. The other two times had been slow, sensual elaborations of all the ways that touch could ignite the soul.

Without a doubt, she had made the best decision of her life in asking Solomon to marry her and in holding fast to her desire to have a real marriage in whatever time they had.

With her head snuggled against Solomon's shoulder, she closed her eyes and attempted to drift off again, but now that she was awake, excitement buzzed through her. She opened her eyes and trailed her fingertips across the firm muscles of her husband's chest. He was such a contrast to her—hard where she was soft, powerful where she was compliant. She loved the differences between them, but what she loved more was the deep-seated feeling that they were alike in all the ways that really mattered.

Her gentle exploration of his chest and stomach eventually drew Solomon out of sleep. His steady breathing hitched and he let out a low rumble of pleasure.

"This is one fine way to greet the new day," he said, turning his head to hers.

Honoria giggled. Heavens, since when had she become the sort to *giggle*? "I agree." She surged forward to lightly kiss his lips, keeping her hand spread flat against his lower abdomen. She wanted so badly to inch her hand lower still to bring that part of him that she instantly cherished alive once more.

He must have felt her desire. With one swift movement, he rolled her to her back, fitting himself between her legs. As badly as she wanted to give herself over to him again, the pointed soreness that his movement caused had her wincing before she could stop herself.

Lucky for her, Solomon chuckled. "I should know better." He bent down to kiss her lingeringly. "I should have known better than to lose my head the way I did last night."

"Oh, no," she was quick to correct him. "It was wonderful." To prove it, she sighed and wriggled against him.

Solomon caught his breath. She could feel him stiffening by the moment between her thighs. "You are a temptress, aren't you?" His eyes were full of humor and hunger.

She laughed. "I never would have thought so, but you make me wild."

His entire expression heated to something so

arousing that Honoria was ready to forget her soreness just to feel him as one with her again.

Instead, Solomon kissed her quickly, then lurched back, climbing out of bed. Honoria caught one, tantalizing glimpse of his erection before he turned away, heading to his wardrobe.

"I could hurt you if we're not careful," he said with a laugh, although Honoria heard far more seriousness in the statement.

She stretched and flexed her sore muscles, loving the sudden rush of cool air against her heated skin. "I don't know that I'd mind at this point."

"Maybe not at this point, but you would when you found yourself trying to do simple household tasks." He selected a suit from the wardrobe then turned back to the bed. His eyes lit with fire as he drank in the sight of her naked and spread across the sheets. Then he laughed and shook his head. "You are too much temptation for this weak man to handle, Honoria Templesmith."

She laughed, then twisted to her side and reluctantly crawled out of bed. He was right about one thing, though. The more she moved and went through basic tasks of washing and dressing for the day, the more she noticed the sweet soreness that their wedding night had left her with. It wasn't the same sort of annoyance as stubbing her toe or burning her hand on a stove. It was a delicious reminder of how exuberantly she and her new husband had gotten to know each other in the night.

"I actually do know how to make breakfast," she said later, when the two of them finally made their way downstairs to the kitchen.

"Do you?" Solomon asked with a smile as he went to the pantry and came out with a tin of already-ground coffee.

"Yes, it was easier to sneak down to the kitchens to help Maria in the morning, before anyone else was up," she explained. There was already a pan for frying bacon and scrambling eggs on the counter from their meal the night before, so she took it to the stove—which Solomon was already adding more wood to—then went in search of eggs and the rest of the bacon. "I can do pancakes as well, and I even learned how to make muffins and scones."

It seemed silly to brag about something so common, but Solomon grinned and looked impressed all the same.

They worked together to fix a hearty breakfast. By the time they were seated at the kitchen table with bacon, eggs, toast, coffee, and ideas for far more elaborate breakfasts in the days to come, Honoria was certain that she'd never been happier in her life. Even if sitting was slightly uncomfortable.

"If I could close up the bank and spend the day with you today, I would," Solomon told her as he speared his last bit of eggs.

"Don't you own the bank?" she asked. "You could set your own hours."

"I could." He nodded, the businesslike expression that made him look even more authoritative coming over him. "But banks are an institution that require a great deal of trust in order to be successful. Perhaps more than anything, a person's money is their life, or at least a crucial part in it. They entrust that bit of their life to me, so it is my duty to both safeguard it and to give the appearance of absolute confidence. That includes making sure the bank maintains regular hours."

"That's very noble of you." Honoria sat straighter. "I'm not sure every banker out there feels the same way."

Solomon shrugged. "It's true. Some men enter banking to make their own fortunes."

"Why did you become a banker?"

A wistful smile pulled at his handsome face. "Because Howard Haskell asked me to."

"Oh?" She blinked. "I didn't realize you knew Howard before you came to Haskell."

"I did, but how we met is a story for another day. The short version is that he knew my background and my capabilities, saw that I was good with money, and sold me on the idea of providing financial services to the new town he was building out West."

Honoria grinned and shook her head. "I've heard so many stories of people who Howard asked to move here specifically so that he could grow his own little Utopia in the high plains. It's a wonder my father ever settled here at all."

"Why did he?"

Honoria shrugged. "Business. He saw that there wasn't much ranching competition and set up his enterprise. It's not that interesting of a story."

"Even so, I'll have to get you to tell me all of it someday." The edges of Solomon's smile faltered as soon as he finished speaking. The same, terrible sadness came to his eyes that had been there every time they talked about time and the future.

The last thing Honoria wanted her new husband to think about the day after their wedding was how short their marriage would be. She stood, forcing a smile, and reached for his plate. "You'd better hurry up and get ready for work, Mr. Templesmith. We don't want your loyal customers to lose confidence in you."

She whisked the plates off to the sink. Solomon stood and followed her. As Honoria reached to work the pump, Solomon closed in on her from behind. His hands caressed her hips, and he bent down to nuzzle the sensitive flesh of her neck. Flutters of longing danced through her at the intimate contact.

"I only care that you have confidence in me, Mrs. Templesmith," he murmured against her ear.

She drew in a deep breath, letting the scent of him fill her lungs. Strange, but she hadn't had a single coughing fit or any tickly hints of one since walking into his house as his bride.

"I do," she said in echo of her wedding vows, twisting to settle herself in his arms. "I have complete confidence in you." It was such a wonderful thing to be able to say, as wonderful as the kiss that followed.

She could have lost herself in kissing him forever, but all too soon, he broke the kiss and straightened. His expression was sunny and casual once more. "And what do you plan to do with yourself on this first day as a married woman?" he asked.

A thrill zipped through Honoria's heart. "I hadn't thought about it." She did now, tilting her head to the side even as she kept her arms circled around his back. "I suppose I should start with decorating your house, since you told me I could."

He laughed. "That sounds like a fine pursuit. I have credit at every store in town, so feel free to put my financial solubility to the test."

Her expression brightened. She'd completely forgotten that Solomon was a wealthy man. As quickly as ideas of everything she could do with his money swooped in on her, she reminded herself that now was not the time to turn into one of her sisters.

"I'll be frugal," she said. "I'd rather decorate for beauty and function than pure ostentation."

"Why am I not surprised?" He grinned and kissed the tip of her nose.

The gesture was so sweet and almost silly that she giggled. Yes, giggling was definitely her new favorite pastime.

Solomon straightened, putting on a mock serious face. "Decorating is all well and good, but what do you plan to do once you're finished? How would you like to spend your time?"

Time. It was the one luxury she most longed for and the only thing she knew she couldn't have.

She took a deep breath and tried not to give in to the gloom that reared up from the place she'd packed it away. "I think…I think that I would like to spend the rest of my time making beautiful things," she said, glancing up into his eyes. "To be remembered by."

The sadness that filled his expression was painful, but he kissed her all the same. "I think that's a fine ambition," he said, almost in a whisper. "We can find ways for you to do that."

At last, he broke away, heading for the table where he'd left his jacket hung over the back of his chair.

"I really should be going."

Honoria wondered if she'd made him so sad he needed to run. Probably. She rushed over to him, helping him put his jacket on, then straightened it when he turned to her. "Have a lovely day, husband," she said, suddenly shy.

He lifted a hand to cradle the side of her face, then tilted it up to kiss her. "You too, wife."

He kissed her one last time, then turned and headed down the hall. Honoria stood and watched him, her heart fluttering like a bird…but like a bird trapped in a cage that knew it couldn't get out. Marrying Solomon had been an act of self-preservation, but it dawned on her that leaving him would be the hardest thing she'd ever done.

The thought was too heavy, so she turned to set about cleaning up their breakfast. Once everything was washed, dried, stored, and put away, she made a tour of the rest of the house, assessing what needed to be bought or improved on. The list became too long to keep mentally, so she found some paper and a pencil and jotted down notes for each room. Finally, as the morning was well on its way, she set out to see what the stores of Haskell had to offer.

She was barely out the door when the cozy world of her new, married life was breached.

"Honoria! What a delight to see you," Estelle Tremaine called out to her as soon as Honoria had rounded the corner onto Station Street. Estelle changed direction to meet her in the middle of the road with a fond hug. "We were all so pleased when word got out yesterday that you and Solomon had married."

"Thank you." Honoria hardly knew what to do, whether to hug Estelle back. As far as she was concerned, the woman hardly knew her, yet here she was greeting her like a sister.

No, not like a sister. Her experience with sisters was something else entirely.

Estelle held her at arm's length, beaming as she studied her. "You look beautiful this morning. Married life must agree with you."

The possibility of having a conversation with a woman from town—a woman who her family did not approve of—made Honoria bold. "It does," she admitted, instantly feeling her cheeks redden.

Estelle must have known exactly what she meant. Of course she did. She herself had been married to Lt. Tremaine for over ten years, and they had several children together. "Well, I won't keep you from your errands, but you must come over for tea with me and some friends soon."

"Tea?" The invitation was as exciting as it was unexpected.

"Yes." Estelle squeezed her hand. "I'll talk to Olivia as soon as she's done with school and we can set a time."

"That would be lovely."

Estelle let her go, but as Honoria walked on, she blinked in wonder. She hadn't done very well for her first conversation with someone she'd admired for years, but Estelle didn't seem to think so.

She was still running over the brief exchange in her mind, wondering what she could have done to sound like less of a ninny, when another lilting voice shook her out of her thoughts.

"Honoria, congratulations!" This time it was Corva Haskell, the wife of Howard's son, Franklin, who stopped her as she made the turn onto Main Street. Corva carried her baby boy, Howard Franklin Haskell, on her hip but still moved quickly enough to join Honoria in her walk up Haskell's central thoroughfare.

"Mrs. Haskell, good morning," Honoria greeted her, determined to do better at conversing this time.

"It's so good to see you walking about town freely." Corva smiled as if she genuinely meant it. But of course she did. Unlike her sisters, when women like Corva gave compliments, they were true and not just masks for later insults or ways to coerce someone into doing something for them. "Are you on your way to the bank to see your husband?" Her eyes danced at the word.

Corva's high spirits were infectious. "No, I'm on my way to do some shopping. Solomon's house is spartan at best."

"I'm certain he picked the perfect woman to decorate

it." Corva winked. "But how you surprised everyone."

"Surprised them?"

"Yes. No one even knew you and Solomon were courting."

"I…" There was no way to even begin the conversation about why she and Solomon had married without giving away far more information than she wanted to.

Lucky for her, she didn't have to say a thing.

"Of course, I imagine you'd have to keep that courtship secret from your father," Corva went on. "He didn't look particularly happy about it at the reception yesterday."

An odd twist struck Honoria's gut. A tiny cough escaped her. "How was he?"

"Livid," Corva admitted with a sympathetic sigh. "Your sisters weren't too pleased either. They refused to let anyone talk about it, and whenever they caught someone whispering about how happy for the two of you they were, Vivian and Melinda railed at them and tossed them out."

"Oh, dear."

Corva hummed in agreement. "Franklin and I had to leave early because of little Howard here, but Miriam Montrose was just telling me this morning about how toward the end, there was hardly anyone left for the cake-cutting."

"Oh, no." Right alongside Honoria's pang of sympathy for her sister was a heaping of embarrassment for how her entire family must have behaved.

"If I were you, I'd thank my lucky stars that your family isn't likely to be in town today," Corva went on. "But I suppose Vivian is enjoying her honeymoon right now."

Honoria hid a grimace. "Cousin Rance didn't want to go on a honeymoon. He said it was too expensive, and who would want to see a bunch of old cities anyhow?"

Corva laughed, not understanding how bitter a point of contention that announcement had been. "What about you?" Her expression lightened. "Are you and Solomon going on a honeymoon?"

Honoria hesitated. It would have been lovely for the two of them to run away to the sea or to the woods, or any place where they could be alone, but there were far too few places in the world that would look kindly on a white woman and a black man holidaying together. That wasn't even taking her health into consideration.

"Solomon feels a great duty of responsibility to his bank," she answered instead, feeling that it was as true as anything. "Perhaps we'll find a way to take a vacation later."

"I certainly hope you do." They reached Kline's mercantile, but Corva continued with, "You must allow Franklin and I to host a small party for you. Maybe lunch or something. I'm sure everyone is dying to hear your story."

First tea with Estelle and her friends, and now lunch with Corva and hers? Had Haskell always been filled with this many sweet, wonderful friends? Of course, she would never have noticed if she was constantly being dragged around by Vivian and Melinda.

Vivian and Melinda.

"There she is!"

It was actually Bebe who yelped like someone who had stuck her with a pin from further down the boardwalk on the other side of the store. Honoria jumped at her sister's voice. Every last inch of her confidence melted to dread at the sight of all three of her sisters marching toward her. They were all dressed like royalty, and Melinda and Bebe held their heads high with haughty grandeur, but Vivian looked downright pale.

"Ugh! I don't ever want to see that traitor again," Vivian spat. All the same, she continued to stride forward, coming to stop in front of Honoria with her arms crossed. Her lips pressed into a tight line. There were dark circles under her eyes, as if she hadn't slept or had been crying.

"Disgusting little vermin." Melinda echoed her posture, chin tilted up.

"Papa's really mad at you," Bebe said in a much quieter, more subdued voice.

"I am aware," Honoria answered. Her mind raced and her heart with it. She did not want to be beaten back into the place she'd escaped from so happily yesterday, but more than a decade of enduring her sisters' wrath made standing up for herself awkward. She took a deep breath, and instantly dissolved into a coughing fit.

"Oh, my. Are you all right?" Corva shifted little Howard against her hip and rested a hand on Honoria's arm.

"She only does that to get attention," Vivian sniffed.

"Yeah, just like she runs off and marries a...a *most* unsuitable man to get attention too," Melinda added.

"I don't think she always does it to get attention," Bebe added quietly.

"Shut up, Bebe," Vivian and Melinda said in unison.

That was enough to shock Honoria out of her coughing. She blinked, glancing from Vivian and Melinda to Bebe, standing one step behind him. "Oh, Bebe, no," she sighed.

"What?" Bebe's back snapped straight, and she imitated Vivian and Melinda's haughty glare.

Wincing, Honoria said, "I'm afraid you'll find out all too soon."

"What's that supposed to mean?" Bebe deflated somewhat.

"How dare you steal my thunder?" Vivian barked before Honoria could answer. "That was supposed to be *my* wedding day."

"It was," Honoria answered plainly.

"Yes, but all anyone could talk about was *you*," Melinda said.

Vivian swatted her. Melinda yelped in protest.

"You conspired to undermine me right from the beginning, I suspect," Vivian said.

"I swear to you, Vivian, it was no conspiracy."

"I don't believe you." She turned her face half away from Honoria.

For a flash of an instant, Honoria caught sight of a round, purple mark on her neck under her high collar. She'd once spied the same sort of mark on the neck of one of their classmates after a boy had been kissing her there.

Vivian caught her staring and instantly slapped a hand to her neck. Her face went red with shame and misery. Uncomfortable pieces of a matrimonial picture started to come together in Honoria's mind, and that picture looked very different from what she'd experienced with Solomon the night before.

"I'm…I'm so sorry, Vivian," she murmured softly, feeling completely out of her depth.

"What?" Vivian growled.

For all the misery Vivian had inflicted on her life, Honoria still felt horrible that whatever her sister had experienced on her wedding night hadn't been enjoyable. She had to help in some way. "It…it's really quite wonderful if you let it be," she fumbled.

Melinda and Bebe's faces went bright red. Vivian's paled even further, taking on a decidedly green hue. "How dare you?" Vivian seethed. Her gaze flickered to Corva, and she took a step closer to wedge her out of the conversation. "How dare you suggest something so filthy and vile in public?"

"I only meant that—"

"I'm not surprised that *you* would disgrace yourself by doing *that* with a man that is little better than an ape!"

Honoria's mouth dropped open. Her hand was halfway raised to slap Vivian the way she'd wanted to for years before sense and decorum got the better of her. She couldn't care less what Vivian said about her. She'd been saying much worse for years. But to insult Solomon—a kind, caring, sensitive gentleman—was too much. She fought back with the sharpest weapon she had.

"I'm not the one who is defective when it comes to the most important duty of a wife."

Instantly, she felt horrible. Not just because of the shock on Melinda and Bebe's face, but because her insult hit its mark hard. Vivian's face pinched to misery and shame, and for the first time in her life, Honoria thought she was on the verge of watching her sister break down into real tears that weren't designed to get her something.

"Vivian, I'm sor—"

"You'd better watch your back." Before Honoria could apologize, Vivian's fury had returned tenfold. She poked a finger into Honoria's arm, hurting as acutely as a bee sting. "Papa is angrier than I've ever seen him before."

"I'm sure." Honoria lowered her head, not in defeat, but because it seemed the safest way to deflect Vivian's spite.

"No." Vivian swayed closer to her still, so close that Honoria had to arch her back to keep from being spit on.

"You don't know the half of it. I've never seen him like this. He hasn't stopped shouting about how far you've fallen and how shamefully you've disgraced yourself by running into that man's arms." She narrowed her eyes. "And now I can tell him how eagerly you flopped onto your back in his bed."

Honoria fought not to lose her balance as Vivian brought her face so close that their noses touched.

"Papa will kill him."

The words reverberated so deeply into Honoria's soul that she stumbled back, only barely catching herself before she fell over. The moment was made worse as she launched into a wracking cough that left her gasping for breath.

Vivian, for her part, had straightened, crossed her arms, and watched her with undisguised malice. Melinda's expression mirrored the spite in Vivian's. Bebe was trying to look just as vicious, but genuine worry ruined her attempt.

"Ladies, you shouldn't say such things," Corva commented from the side.

"They're true," Melinda said with deadly seriousness, continuing to stare at Honoria.

It took Honoria far longer than it ever had to recover from her coughing spell. She clutched at her chest and had to accept Corva's help to remain upright. A huge part of her wanted to argue that their father was not that sort of man, that he wouldn't resort to murder simply because he was angry. But she knew him too well. She knew his temper and she knew his prejudices. She'd married Solomon because she wanted a few moments of happiness before she died, but she hadn't stopped to consider that she might be taking Solomon to the grave with her.

"We have shopping to do," Vivian said at last tilting

her head and putting on a vicious smile as though she'd won some game. "Come on, Melinda. You too, Bebe."

Melinda looked at Honoria down her nose, then "hmphed," and followed Vivian into Kline's mercantile. Bebe took longer to follow. She stared at Honoria with an open mouth, worry furrowing her brow.

"I don't think he's really capable of killing anyone," she said quickly, gulping at the end.

"I don't either," Honoria said.

But she only said that to comfort her youngest sister. In her heart, she knew her father was capable of murder if the victim was Solomon.

# Chapter Seven

The only thing out of the ordinary at the bank that day was the fact that Solomon couldn't pay attention to his work to save his life. Every set of numbers he tried to figure tangled up and faded away as he indulged in daydreams of his new wife.

Honoria was everything he could ever have hoped for and more. She'd touched his heart years ago with her kind disposition and her endurance in the face of a family that treated her shamefully, but he never would have guessed at her boldness or her willingness to learn about everything from cookery to passion.

He sat at his desk in the back of the bank, gazing into nothing as he remembered how eagerly she'd responded to his touch, how freely she had given voice to her pleasure, and how lovingly she'd accepted him. The very memory of the night did things to him physically that he would do best to fight against. The bank wasn't crowded, but it was a public place.

His thoughts were still soaring as he strode home that evening, his steps faster than usual.

"You gonna stop in for a drink?" Sam called from the door to the saloon as Solomon passed. The clever grin he wore betrayed that his question wasn't serious, that he knew the answer.

"Not when I have a beautiful wife waiting for me," Solomon called back. He tipped his hat and went on his way, a little bit of a strut in his walk.

Every ounce of sunshine that had filled his soul all day crashed when he walked through his front door only to find Honoria sitting hunched up in a ball on the stairs.

"Sweetheart, what's wrong?" He rushed to her, reaching out to take her in his arms as she stood. The terrible thought that her illness was suddenly much worse when he had secretly thought she seemed so much better struck him.

"Oh, Solomon, I'm so worried." She threw her arms around him and buried her face against his shoulder.

"Worried?" He embraced her tightly. As much as he wanted to reassure her, there were a thousand things she could be justifiably worried about.

It was a few more moments until her breathing calmed and she lifted her head to say, "I ran into my sisters in town earlier."

Solomon frowned. "Why would they all be in town after Vivian's wedding yesterday?"

A sweet blush came to Honoria's cheeks and she lowered her eyes. "Apparently Vivian didn't enjoy her wedding night as much as I did."

In spite of the other implication, Solomon's chest swelled with pride.

"But that's not what worries me," she rushed on before he could make any sort of silly, vain comment about her enjoying him. The way Honoria's blushed drained away, leaving her pale with anxiety meant it was no time for jokes. "Papa isn't happy with me."

"I expect not." He shifted so that he could rest his hand on the side of her face, running a comforting thumb over her cheek. "There's nothing he can do to us. Our marriage is legal in Haskell, thanks to Howard's forward thinking. He can't force you to go home." He finished his reassurance with a light kiss.

Honoria didn't look relieved. In fact, her misery appeared to have doubled. She was having a hard time meeting his eyes. "There are far worse things Papa could do than try to have our marriage dissolved."

The way she spoke, the tension in her shoulders, the race of the pulse in her neck so near to his fingers…he wasn't fool enough to miss what that could mean.

"I've faced more than my fair share of prejudice, Honoria," he told her seriously. "I know how to protect myself, and I swear that I will protect you as well."

Her eyes darted up to meet his. "Vivian implied that Papa might try to kill you," she whispered.

He smiled. It was a bitter, gallows smile, but it was the response he'd learned to have to those sorts of threats. "Let him try. This is not the first time that my life has been threatened."

Honoria blinked, rocking back, horrified. "It's not?"

He shook his head. "Plenty of folks don't like to see a man of color succeeding in this world. I've lost track of the number of times someone has tried to put me down."

"But death threats, Solomon." She clutched the front of his suit as if she could drag him away from danger by his lapels.

"They're just threats, and all threats can be guarded against."

"Are you sure?" She didn't look at all convinced.

He was glad she never had to deal with this sort of

hate, as glad as he was frustrated that she had to deal with it now. Honoria didn't deserve to be in danger for one moment.

"Sweetheart, as long as you're safe, then your father can rattle his saber at me all he wants. I've made it this far, and I'll make it even farther."

He pressed his hands over top of hers as they held onto his jacket. Her tension lessened by a hair, and she nodded. The worry was still in her eyes, and probably deeper. Solomon fought it by folding her against his chest in a protective embrace. He stood there with her, waiting until her body loosened and she sagged against him.

"By any chance have you fixed supper?" he asked at length.

She shook her head against his shoulder.

"Good." He nodded, setting her away from him. "I was hoping you'd say that. I want to treat you to supper at the hotel."

"But…but are you sure that's a good idea?" The way she bit her lip would have been sensual if she wasn't so anxious. "I mean, people might see us. They might talk."

Solomon laughed. "Are you saying that after seeking me out and asking me to marry you, sneaking behind your family's back at your sister's wedding to have the ceremony, and giving yourself to me last night so freely, you're embarrassed to be seen eating supper with me?"

"No, that's not what I meant at all." Her cheeks flared such a deep red that Solomon's heart beat in double-time.

"Then come along, beautiful wife of mine." He turned and took Honoria's arm, placing her hand in the crook of his elbow. "Let's walk through all of Haskell together and let everyone see us as we enjoy a fine meal."

She didn't protest, but for a moment it looked like she might. They headed out the front door and around the corner to Station Street to take the most public route to the hotel.

"I was going to tell you how I met Howard Haskell and accepted his invitation to open a bank in town," he said as they walked.

His ploy worked. Honoria turned to him, eyes bright with interest. "How did you?"

Solomon settled into a satisfied smile. He walked at a stately pace. "I worked for him for a time in his financial office in Cincinnati, Ohio. But for that story to make sense, I have to tell you how I ended up there in the first place."

"Yes, I was going to ask."

He hesitated, searching for the best way to tell his story. It wasn't the first time he'd told it, but it was the first time he'd told a woman. Some things had to have their edges smoothed so as not to hurt delicate sensibilities. Not that Honoria was delicate, per se.

"I was born a slave on a cotton plantation in Alabama," he got right to it. "One of the largest plantations in Limestone County. But for one lucky twist of fate, my story would have been no different than any other story of a plantation slave."

"What was that?" Honoria held tightly to his arm, absorbed in his story. A few people they passed stared at them, but she didn't notice.

"My mother was a house slave, chosen for the position because she was beautiful," he went on. "She was able to keep me near her when I was young, and as a result, I became a playmate to the master's son, Martin."

"Oh." Honoria blinked. "I didn't realize that happened."

"It does, or did." He smiled at her. Maybe someday he'd tell her all of the not-so-pretty details about dynamics on a plantation. "What did not usually happen was for that sort of friendship to last beyond the early days of childhood. Martin and I felt more like brothers than anything. Of course, his father disapproved." That was an understatement. He'd tried several times to sell Solomon to a different plantation, to no avail.

"Martin was far more progressive than his father knew. He was an avid reader, and a secret abolitionist, though it made no sense for him to be one."

"Why not?"

"Because he was set to inherit that plantation."

They turned the corner onto Main Street. Most of the town's businesses had closed for the day or were in the process of closing, but several people were still out and about.

"Martin saw which way the wind was blowing. He knew that war was coming. About a year before hostilities broke out, he invented an excuse to go on a trip up North, to Philadelphia. He insisted on taking me with him to act as valet, as he said."

Honoria frowned. "And he got away with that excuse?"

Solomon shrugged. "I'm not sure that he told his father what he was doing. By that point, the old man was gravely ill. It was more of a challenge to make our way up along the Mississippi River and then across Ohio and Pennsylvania by train. There were a few close calls, and I was almost mistaken for a fugitive slave and abducted at one point."

"Oh, no." She hugged his arm.

"Martin explained my position and got me out of trouble." He said a quick prayer of thanks to his old friend. "When we reached Philadelphia, he officially set me free. More than that, he provided for my education. You see, at that time, Philadelphia was one of the only cities in the nation that had an institute of higher learning for freedmen, one set up by the Quakers."

"How forward-thinking of them." Honoria smiled. "And for your friend to grant you your freedom."

He glanced to her, returning her smile. "It *was* forward-thinking and wonderful, but it was also part self-preservation. Martin had run away from home too, you see. I could still have been captured as a fugitive slave and him as a criminal. Martin could only take so much money with him, so we shared lodgings while we both attended college and worked. We both studied law. We had each other's back when the war broke out and Martin's loyalties were questioned. Back then, a man who didn't join the army was treated as miserably as a man of color trying to better himself."

"I suppose he couldn't join the army," Honoria figured. "He was a citizen of the Confederacy living in the Union, right?"

"That's how Martin justified it, yes. But he was hated for it." Solomon himself had resented the way the man who had more or less saved his life was treated. He rushed on. "The war ended, we both graduated, and both of us found jobs. It was easier for Martin. He took up work with a firm in New York City, and he's still there today."

"Oh! I'm delighted to hear he's still doing well."

Solomon nodded. "We write to each other, but he has a family now and my life has changed so much. It began to change in earnest when I moved to Cincinnati to take up the only position working in the law that I could find. Mind you, they wouldn't let me sit the bar exam."

"They wouldn't?"

He grinned at her faith in him and her innocence over matters of prejudice. "No. I ended up working at a clerk in the office of a law firm that worked mostly with business clientele. One of our clients was a certain Mr. Howard Haskell. He was young and untested. The office didn't take either of us seriously, so I was assigned to his account." He grinned. "That twist of fate might have been even more important to the course of my life than being born the son of a house slave."

"Really?"

They were nearing the top of Main Street, close to the bank and the intersection with Elizabeth Street. More and more people craned their necks to get a look at them as they passed. A few of their friends waved.

"I learned about the law in college, but Howard taught me all about money. And believe me, there's no one you want to learn about money from more than Howard. He encouraged me to invest my savings, and when that investment bore fruit, he guided me in ways to reinvest the profits. I studied everything he did, mimicked it, and before long, I had more money than anyone at my law firm would have dreamed of."

"How clever." Her smile of pride warmed his heart.

"What was even more clever was not letting on that I had so much money," he continued. "I kept that a closely guarded secret. It wasn't until Howard sent me a letter inviting me to come help settle Haskell and to be its banker that I let on to anyone how much my investments had earned or who was the holder of most of the stocks and notes that I had. I only really started living this kind of life when I arrived here."

"Because no one here would care one way or another about the fortune that a man of color made for himself," Honoria finished his thought. Her logic surprised him. Maybe he'd underestimated her after all. But of course he had. Honoria was far more intelligent than anyone suspected.

"The beauty of Haskell is that it was invented out of Howard's vision for the world he wanted to live in," he continued. "Howard is unique in that he sees people for their virtues, not their appearance. So when you tell me you're worried about what your father might do, I share your concern, but I have faith in this uncommon spot that Howard has created." He placed his free hand over hers in his elbow. "I have faith that even if the worst attempts are made, there are enough people here who would stand up for me, stand up for us, that it would all come to nothing."

"I can only pray that you're right," Honoria said. The lines furrowing her brow smoothed and her smile warmed. "You've led quite a life, Solomon Templesmith."

Solomon chuckled. They'd reached the corner of the hotel, so he slowed his steps. "No more so than anyone who has wanted to end up in a better place than he started."

She paused and shifted to take his hands. "Whatever else, whatever troubles might come our way, I'm proud to be married to you." Her words made him feel like the tallest man in the world, even when she added, "For however long we have."

He didn't want to think about this beautiful thing between them ever coming to an end, so instead he focused on their more immediate problem. "Honoria, if your father continues to be a problem, if you ever feel unsafe or anxious—"

"Well, lookie here, boys."

The timing of the sour call from further down Elizabeth Street was so shockingly, bitterly apropos that Solomon winced. He let go of Honoria's hands and turned to face the approaching threat. Four men in the dusty clothes of ranch hands were strolling toward them.

"It's the boss's daughter and her n— husband," another of the men barked.

"No," Honoria whispered.

Solomon shifted to block her from the snarling ranch hands. "What do you boys want?"

"*Boys*?" The first one, Ted, snorted. Solomon recognized each of the men who worked for Rex. They kept their money in his bank, after all.

"Where do *you* get off calling *us* boys?" Kyle, the one who had called him the dirty name, followed.

"Seems like if anyone here should be called 'boy' it's a jumped-up slave like you," Wayne added, then spit.

People were beginning to stir on the hotel's front porch. Some of them strained forward to watch the confrontation while others dashed inside.

"The term wasn't meant to give offense," Solomon explained in measured tones. "Now if you will all excuse me, I've come to take my wife to dinner at the hotel." He touched the brim of his hat. The deadly expression he wore was the real message, though.

Rex's hands didn't get that message.

"I always thought the boss's daughters were fine ladies," Keith, the last one to speak but, in Solomon's experience, the most vicious, said. "I had no idea that this one was a darkie-loving whore."

A few of the observers on the porch gasped in offense. Honoria swayed closer to Solomon, grasping for his hand. It was a good thing she did. If he'd had his hands free, Solomon would have punched the man's foul mouth so hard that he'd rattle when he walked from all the teeth in his stomach.

"You need to beg my wife's pardon," he said in a low, dangerous voice.

"I ain't begging for nothing from a filthy whore." Keith narrowed his eyes, stepping closer.

"Ignore him," Honoria whispered, squeezing Solomon's hand. "He's too stupid to bother fighting with."

"I'm not asking you to apologize," Solomon growled. "I'm telling you."

"Boss wouldn't like it if you got his daughter into a fight," Ted murmured.

"Oh, I don't think he'd mind at all," Keith seethed, his eyes never leaving Solomon's. "He's madder 'n a hornet in hell about this one spoiling herself. Seems to me he'd thank us for doing him the favor of saving him the trouble of dealing with it."

"If anyone will be dealt with, it will be you gentlemen," Solomon said. Out of the corner of his eye he spotted Theophilus Gunn rushing out to the porch. "Only a blackguard insults a lady."

The four hands laughed and traded sneers. "You have no idea what Rex's got in store for you," Kyle said.

A bolt of alarm hit Solomon's gut. These four were child's play to deal with. If Rex truly was intent on some sort of revenge, it could be a problem. Judging by the smug grins that his cronies wore, he'd be lucky if he could provide Honoria with the peace he'd intended to.

"Rex Bonneville had better think twice about causing trouble," he said, knowing his words would fall on deaf ears. "He might find that he brings more harm to himself than to me."

As expected, the four men snorted and guffawed.

"Mr. Templesmith," Gunn spoke from the top of the stairs. "Your table in the restaurant is ready for you and your lovely wife whenever you're ready for it."

The sharp look for Rex's hands that accompanied the otherwise mild comment was as dangerous as if Gunn had pointed a rifle at each of them. No one in town was quite sure what it was about the mild, white-haired man, but that unnamable something marked him as a man no one wanted to mess with. Keith and the others lost some of their swagger as they shifted as far away from Gunn's stare as they could.

"You ain't heard the last of this," Keith growled as he passed Solomon and Honoria. The four men continued down Elizabeth Street, likely heading to either the Silver Dollar saloon or Bonnie's place. Wayne spit near Solomon's feet as he passed.

Because he missed, Solomon ignored him. He slid his arm around Honoria's waist and ushered her up the hotel stairs to where Gunn stood.

"See," Honoria whispered. "This was why I was worried. This is exactly what my sisters were talking about."

Solomon shook his head. "I can handle bullies like those four."

"But can you handle Rex Bonneville?" Gunn asked, joining them to walk inside the hotel.

"Yes," Solomon answered unequivocally.

Neither Gunn nor Honoria looked as certain.

"I shouldn't have done this," Honoria sighed, biting her lip. "I shouldn't have put you in danger."

"Sweetheart," Solomon stopped her, turning to her and taking her face in his hands. "I am so glad that you did that there will never be words enough to express it. I made promises to you—when I asked you to marry me, when we stood in front of Rev. Pickering in the church, and in my heart every moment that we've been together since. I will cherish and make good on those promises."

She smiled up at him, her eyes glassy with tears.

Solomon wasn't sure if he loved her smile or hated that the tears were there to mar it.

"You're a good and noble man, Solomon," Gunn cut in from the side. "But do you think you might want some sort of protection until the situation resolves? I could arrange for some old associates to come to town to monitor your house and business."

Solomon's brow flew up at the suggestion—not just because Gunn was generous for offering it, but because he knew people who could act as bodyguards in the first place. The mysteries surrounding the man would fill a library.

"No," he said at last. "I can take care of myself."

"Are you sure?" Gunn asked. The same question was in Honoria's eyes.

Solomon turned his head to study his wife for a moment. "Yes," he answered at last. "There's nothing those hooligans could do that I fear. And as for Rex, let him do his worst."

# *Chapter Eight*

Honoria had no appetite for her supper, even though it looked and smelled delicious. She couldn't shake the feeling that she'd done something far worse than she'd ever done by thinking only of herself and putting Solomon in danger with this marriage. No matter how much he protested that that wasn't the case. In fact, the only thing that unraveled the tension in her muscles and made her forget there was any sort of lingering danger was when Solomon took her home, undressed her, and kept her up half the night exploring new and amazing ways to lose themselves in each other's arms.

But by the time morning rolled around, the worries were back threefold.

"I swear to you, Honoria, it will be all right," Solomon told her as they sat across the breakfast table from each other.

Honoria dragged her troubled expression up to meet his confident one. She'd barely touched the blueberry pancakes she'd made, though Solomon had scarfed down so many that she wasn't sure where he was putting them all. At least that thought smoothed away part of the rough edges around her heart.

"I mean it." He reached across the table, taking her hand.

His expression turned stern and thoughtful for a moment. He truly was a beautiful man. Even frowning, the strong lines of his cheekbones and jaw made him stand out. He'd only just shaved, so the planes of his cheeks were smooth. Honoria caught herself wanting to touch them…just as she wanted to touch every part of him…just as she *had* touched every part of him last night. She could spend hours simply running her hands—and perhaps her mouth—over every inch of him.

If Solomon noticed the hot blush that came to her cheeks at the thought, he didn't let on. "I have an idea," he said.

Honoria sat straighter. "Oh?"

Certainty made him seem twice as large and solid as he was. "Yes. Why don't you come to the bank with me today?"

"Me? To the bank?" Actually, the thought thrilled her.

"You're worried about me, and something tells me you won't rest easy until you see that I'm not in any danger. Furthermore, I could teach you how a bank works. I'll even teach you how to work at the teller's window, if you'd like."

The burst of joy that filled her was completely unexpected. "Like a job? I've never had a job before."

Solomon grinned. "Well, here's your chance."

It didn't take much more convincing than that. He was right to think that she would feel better if she saw that he wasn't in any danger at his bank. They cleaned up from breakfast together, then Honoria went upstairs to fix her hair and to make sure she looked bank-ly for the day.

Her confidence was shattered all over again as they walked to the bank. As they headed up Main Street, there was already a small crowd of rough-looking men loitering by the front door.

"It's nothing," Solomon assured her. "Sometimes people who need to make a deposit or a withdrawal arrive before I do."

Maybe, but one look told Honoria that the men waiting worked for her father. All except for Cody and Mason Montrose. The two brothers stood on either side of the door with their arms crossed. They didn't have weapons as far as Honoria could see, but after everything Mr. Gunn had said before supper the night before, she wondered if they were there at his request.

"Morning, gentlemen." Solomon tipped his hat to the Montrose brothers and Rex's workers as he escorted Honoria through them. "The bank will be open in just a moment."

"It'd better be," one of the ranch hands said. None of the men standing there were the ones they had encountered the night before. These ones were the grunt workers who Rex hired to do the menial jobs on the ranch. Honoria barely knew their names, but she knew their looks. None of it was reassuring.

"You need any help in there?" Mason asked as Solomon took out his key and unlocked the door.

Solomon arched his brow and replied, "I'll let you know."

Mason nodded.

"We'll just be hanging around out here if you need anything," Cody said, making it clear to the others that he had his eye on them.

"Thank you, boys," Solomon said.

The lock clicked, and Solomon pushed open the door, whisking Honoria inside. He shut it firmly behind her.

"Mr. Templesmith, thank God you're here!" Solomon's assistant, Mr. Greeley, rushed forward from the long counter that served as the bank's main transaction area.

Most banks had that area barred off from the front lobby, but there was nothing in Solomon's bank to separate the customers from the bank employees. Honoria had never felt as though it was needed until now.

"Those men showed up just as I arrived to count the drawer this morning," Mr. Greeley went on. "They don't look too friendly."

Solomon raised his hand and walked to the side of the counter, unlocking the gate and escorting Honoria through to the back part of the office. "They won't cause any harm, Horace." he assured him.

Mr. Greeley sent Honoria a wary look, as if he knew exactly what had prompted them to be there in the first place. "Congratulations on your nuptials, Mrs. Templesmith," he said, but without the enthusiasm one would have expected.

"Thank you," Honoria answered graciously all the same.

"How soon will we be ready to open?" Solomon let go of Honoria's arm and strode over to Mr. Greeley's side. He peered over the man's shoulder at the ledger that sat open beside a drawer of cash.

"Any time," Mr. Greeley answered with a shrug. "We've got a reasonable amount of cash on hand. Not as much as usual, since we sent off that deposit to San Francisco."

When Honoria frowned in confusion, Solomon turned to explain, "A bank is more than just a safe to lock money away in. Folks deposit their hard-earned cash with us, but instead of having it sit here, I invest it. The investments turn a profit, and that's how I'm able to pay interest on accounts."

"I see." Honoria nodded, coming closer to get a look at Mr. Greeley's ledger. It made sense, and any other day she would have been far more interested in the process.

"Haskell isn't exactly a financial hub," Solomon went on. "I have accounts in San Francisco and New York City, not to mention a wide portfolio of investments. Theoretically, we have enough money to—"

His explanation was cut off by loud rapping on the door. "Open up in there!" Someone shouted. "We want our money."

Solomon tensed. Mr. Greeley looked as though he might jump out of his skin.

"Might as well do what they say," Solomon sighed.

He took Honoria's hand and walked her back to the large desk at the back of the room. Mr. Greeley swallowed and walked around the counter, through the locking gate, and over to the front door.

"I keep track of all of my investments and accounts in this book." Solomon did his best to distract her by inviting her to sit at his desk and taking a huge ledger off of a shelf beside him, but it was no use. Honoria's eyes and attention were firmly on the front door.

As soon as Mr. Greeley opened it, her father's men pushed through. One of them nearly knocked Mr. Greeley over in the process. Mr. Greeley only barely managed to scuttle back through the gate—locking it loudly as he went—and around to his spot near the cash drawer before the burly man in front demanded, "Give me my money!"

"Y-yes, sir," Mr. Greeley stammered. "Right away. If

you'll just fill out this withdrawal form with your name and account number."

Much to Honoria's surprise, her father's worker did as he was asked. They all did. Mr. Greeley handed out forms as the men lined up at the counter to fill them out. Nothing about their aggressive orderliness made her feel a lick better, though.

"See here," Solomon said, still desperately trying to distract her, although his dark frown kept returning to the counter too. "Here are the accounts I have in San Francisco, and here are the ones in New York City."

"A-are these stocks or other sorts of accounts?" she managed to ask, drawing on the minimal financial knowledge she had.

"A little of everything," Solomon answered.

"That's quite a bit of money."

"It's not as much as I'd like it to be, but I'm working on it. Given a few more years—"

"I said I want all of it!" One of Rex's workers raised his voice.

Mr. Greeley stammered wordlessly for a moment. He had a box with file cards in front of him. Several had been pulled and arranged on the desk in front of him.

"All of it is over a hundred dollars, Mr. Jones. Are you sure you want to carry around that much money in cash?"

"Yes," Jones barked. "Give it."

"I want all of mine too," another of the men spoke up. "I got sixty-three dollars and forty-two cents in here. I know. I keep track myself." He held up a rough notepad.

"Yes, sir, Mr. Bueller."

Solomon's frown darkened to a dangerous scowl. He straightened, forgetting everything he was explaining.

Lips pursed in a hard line, he walked up to the desk and peered over Mr. Greeley's shoulder.

"Y'ain't grinning now, are ye?" The man, Jones, sneered at Solomon. "Without your money, you're not anything but a monkey in a suit."

A cold shiver slithered down Honoria's back. Those words sounded very much like something her father would say.

"Gentlemen." Solomon nodded at them, not taking the bait they dangled in front of him. He did, however, take the register Mr. Greeley had been filling out before they came in and returned to the desk with it.

"Is everything all right?" Honoria whispered, hoping he would reassure her once again that, yes, it was.

Solomon set the register on the desk. Honoria rose so that he could take the chair. She leaned over his shoulder once he was seated. He pointed at the final number on the list of figures. It was an impressive one thousand three hundred and twenty-nine dollars, but Honoria still wasn't reassured. Even less so when Solomon took a pencil and a scrap of paper, wrote "$1,329" at the top, then subtracted $114.65 and $63.42.

Honoria pressed a hand to her stomach. A moment later, she burst into coughing. That forced her to step back, but she'd already seen everything she needed to see and knew the consequences. Solomon only had so much cash on hand. If everyone who had deposited their money with him came in and demanded to withdraw everything, it was only a matter of time before the bank ran out of ready cash.

"It can't be as bad as all that," she whispered, resting a hand on Solomon's shoulder. "My father only has so many ranch hands, and he doesn't pay them *that* much."

But she underestimated how far her father would go

for revenge. The first wave of his ranch hands came and went, leaving the bank over four hundred dollars poorer. For a moment, everything settled. But within an hour, one of the smaller ranchers whose land adjoined the Bonneville ranch came in and demanded his entire savings of six hundred dollars. Not even an hour had gone by, and suddenly the bank was in real danger of running out of money.

"Well," Solomon commented grimly as he and Mr. Greeley quickly counted the bank's cash on hand after the rancher left, "you're certainly learning all about banking this morning."

Honoria couldn't tell if he was joking. It was hardly the time to joke.

"Maybe we should invest in building that vault so we can keep more money on hand after all," Mr. Greeley sighed. He counted the last bill and added, "Three hundred and six dollars."

"We might be able to make it." Solomon rubbed his jaw.

The front door opened, and a grumpy-looking tradesman stomped in. "I want to withdraw my money."

Solomon and Mr. Greeley exchanged a look as Mr. Greeley took another withdrawal slip from its cubby. "We might have to close the bank early," he mumbled.

Solomon shook his head. "We absolutely can't. That's what Rex wants. Closing the bank early will damage its reputation and open the way for investigation by state authorities. We have to remain open at all costs."

"But if you run out of cash?" Honoria whispered.

"Give me my money now." The tradesman banged on the counter, prompting Mr. Greeley to move faster, his hands shaking.

Solomon took Honoria's arm and drew her away from the counter. "I guess you were right to be worried," he said with a grim smile. "But you were anxious about the wrong thing. There are more ways to hurt a man than physically."

Honoria's stomach sank. He was partially right. She still wouldn't put it past her father to murder Solomon for marrying her. "What can you do?" she asked.

Solomon leaned back, rubbing his face and sighing. Honoria could practically see his thoughts spinning, and see that he didn't like the conclusion he came to. He grimaced, growled at the back of his throat, then said, "I need you to run over to Howard's office. It's his day to be in town instead of at his ranch. That's probably why Cody and Mason are here."

Relieved to have something to do, Honoria nodded quickly. "What should I say?"

Solomon's wince grew, as if swallowing something bitter. "Ask how much cash he can loan me."

Hope flooded through Honoria as she saw where he was going. "Do you think he has enough?"

"If anyone does, it's Howard."

She nodded. "Right. I'll be back as fast as I can."

She turned to rush off, then at the last moment swung back to Solomon. Heart bursting with pride and something far more tender, she lifted to her toes and kissed him square on the lips. That managed to bring a wistful smile to his face. It was all she could ask for. She whirled away and dashed for the counter and out through the gate.

Howard Haskell's office was part of the town hall complex. He'd built it a few years after Haskell's founding, and had modeled the whole thing on the Capitol Building in Washington D.C. It was a slightly ridiculous piece of grandeur for a small, frontier town, but as Honoria lifted her skirts to rush up the steps, she was comforted by its grandness. Surely someone who had used their own money to finance such an elaborate project would be able to help a friend in trouble.

"Honoria?" Howard glanced up from his desk as Honoria dashed into his office. The door was always open, and Howard didn't believe in having a secretary or anyone to keep people out, even though he was mayor. "What brings you here this morning?"

"It's Solomon," she panted, clutching a hand to her chest to catch her breath. "There's trouble at the bank,"

She explained as fast as she could, only hesitating when it came to asking Howard to bring as much cash as he could to the bank as quickly as possible. Howard listened with grave attention. He didn't seem at all surprised, but luckily for her and for Solomon, he didn't balk at the request for help either.

"I'd say we're all fortunate that I haven't gotten around to making this deposit yet," he said, rising from his desk and crossing the room to a closet.

Honoria tip-toed after him. She felt a little awkward to stand there and watch as he worked the combination on a small safe tucked in the back of the closet, but her awkwardness melted into relief as he took out a fat handful of bills.

"We'll take this to him right away and deposit it so that everything looks aboveboard," he explained, tucking the bills into a pocket inside of his jacket. The pile was so large that he could only fit so much in the pocket. The rest he stuffed into his trousers. Under the circumstances, Honoria didn't think Solomon would mind. "This is all I have on hand, though," Howard continued, striding over to take Honoria's arm and lead her back out to the hall and on outside. "If your father pulls out all the stops, we could be in more trouble."

They hurried back to the bank only to find two more small ranchers had come in to make withdrawals. Honoria had never seen anything like the relief on Solomon's face when she and Howard walked through the doors.

"Pardon me, gentlemen, I have a deposit to make," Howard boomed with all of his good-natured joviality, pushing his way in front of the ranchers.

Howard had brought over three thousand dollars in cash with him. Honoria could hardly believe her eyes as Mr. Greeley counted it all out and tucked it safely into the cash drawer. She had never thought higher than twenty or occasionally fifty dollars at a time for purchases. Suddenly working with such huge sums of cash made her head spin and her heart pound. But both Solomon and Howard seemed used to it.

"What do you plan to do if that isn't enough?" Howard murmured to Solomon, meeting him at the far end of the counter near the gate as the ranchers made their withdrawals.

Solomon sighed, pushing a hand through his short hair. "I don't know. I suppose I'll have to liquidate some of my investments."

Howard nodded grimly. "Gunn will be able to help."

"But only so much," Solomon answered. "And everything depends on how far Bonneville's influence extends." He sent a sideways look to Honoria.

She felt it as if he'd pierced her with an arrow. "This is all my fault." She stepped up to the gate, heart bleeding.

"Nonsense!" Howard boomed.

"You know it isn't." Solomon slipped his arm around her, drawing her closer. "Your father has had it in for me for years. At best, you're the straw that broke the camel's back."

"I would give anything for it not to break at all," she said, laying a hand on his chest.

Solomon smiled and kissed her lightly. "And I wouldn't change a single thing we've done in the last week."

The sudden, powerful urge to tell Solomon that she loved him—not just temporarily or for pretend—swept through Honoria. The idea was scandalous, shameless. She couldn't go loving a man who she'd married for convenience and who she would leave all too soon, and it was better for him if he didn't develop any feelings for her beyond affectionate friendship. If she could have taken things back, she would have spared him even feeling too much affection for her.

"Well, there is one bit of luck we can be thankful for," Howard interrupted her heart's anguish.

"What's that?" she asked, then cleared her throat and stepped a reasonable distance away from her husband.

Howard gave her a lopsided smile. "Your father doesn't do his banking here."

"He doesn't?" Her brow rose in surprise.

"No," Solomon said with a huge measure of relief in his voice, as if he too was just realizing how lucky he was. "Like I said, he's had it in for me for years, so he takes his money all the way to Everland, to their bank."

"And since that amount is likely considerable, he can't ruin you by withdrawing it all at once."

Honoria let out a breath. "That is fortunate."

But just because he didn't do his banking at Solomon's bank didn't mean he wouldn't show his face there. An hour or so later, after Howard had gone back to work and the rush of men coming in to withdraw their funds had slowed, Rex himself strode through the bank doors.

Honoria was on high alert the moment she heard his sharp tenor say, "Well, if this isn't a sorry sight, I don't know what is."

She'd only just come back from the hotel, where she'd gone to fetch Solomon lunch, knowing she wouldn't have time to learn to cook something herself. They were halfway through the meal, but at the sound of her father's voice, Honoria lost her appetite.

"The criminal and his victim sitting down to a cozy meal together," Rex went on.

Honoria and Solomon both stood. Honoria rushed toward him first. "I know what you did here, Papa."

"Of course you do." Rex shrugged. "I make no secret of the fact that I've spread the story of this ape's misdeeds throughout the county." Solomon strode up to stand protectively behind Honoria, but Rex went on. "I freely admit that I encouraged them to withdraw their funds from this sorry excuse for a bank."

"How could you, Papa?" Honoria wasn't sure if she was more heartbroken or angry.

He didn't answer her. He barely looked at her. Instead, he turned a smug grin on Solomon. "I expect you'll be forced to close your doors early. The Wyoming Stock Growers Association won't look too kindly on that."

Honoria's heart stopped in her chest. Solomon scowled. Everyone in Wyoming knew that, while there was a fine government in place in Cheyenne, it was really the WSGA that ran the show in the state. The government was merely a puppet for the WSGA getting what they wanted. And no one regulated the WSGA but themselves.

"As it happens," Solomon answered with cool calm, his back straight, "the bank has been able to fulfill every withdrawal request we've had. We will not be closing early."

Rex's grin faltered. "What?"

"Everyone has been given their money," Honoria answered. "This plan of yours won't work." She wasn't sure what prompted her to say the last bit, but she was glad she did. It actually felt good to stand up to her father.

"We'll see about that," Rex growled. At last, his gaze turned to Honoria. "I'm giving you one last chance," he said, eyes narrowed. "Come home at once."

"No, Papa."

His scowl darkened. "Don't you disobey me, you ungrateful chit. Come home at once! Leave this ridiculous villain and come back to where you belong."

"No," Honoria answered again. She took a step closer to Solomon, reaching for his hand. "Solomon is my husband."

"He is not," Rex sneered. "He's a colored fool who seems to have forgotten that it's illegal to marry a white woman."

"Not in Haskell, it's not," Honoria fired back.

"What kind of life do you plan to have?" Rex shouted. "You take one step outside of this ludicrous town and the authorities will arrest him and drag him to the nearest tree so fast that he won't have time to blubber out a prayer to save him."

"You overestimate the number of people who share your antiquated ideas in this part of the country," Solomon answered. But there was enough tension in his voice and body for Honoria to sense that her father was right to some extent.

The only thing he was wrong about was to ask what kind of a life she planned to have. She had no life in front of her at all. That was the only thing that kept her from crumpling in misery over the position she'd put Solomon in.

"I'm not returning to your ranch with you," she said to fight off the twin waves of gloom and heartache that attacked her. "Solomon's home is my home now, and I will stay with him until the end."

Her father missed the important part of her declaration—the end. He glared at her, jaw clenched. His expression turned deadly as he glanced to Solomon. "So be it," he growled. "I know what I have to do."

Without waiting for a reply, he whipped around and stormed out of the bank. Honoria didn't feel an ounce of relief as he left. The opening salvos had been fired. The war was on.

# Chapter Nine

There were only so many things a bank could do to protect itself from its own customers if they wanted to withdraw their funds.

"The railroad stocks sold quickly," Solomon reported as Honoria lay in bed with him several days later. "I hate to see them go, though. They were some of the fastest-growing stocks I had."

"Will you be able to buy them up again when the crisis passes?" Honoria asked. She curled against his side, one leg stretched over his, tracing small circles on his bare chest as her head rested on his shoulder. The question she really wanted to ask was "Will it be enough?"

"Oh, I'll be able to buy just about everything back again," he replied, running his fingertips along her bare arm. "But at what price, I don't know. Part of the brilliance of some of those investments was catching them when the price of the stock was incredibly low. I won't get nearly as much for my money when I repurchase things, if I can."

She wouldn't have been worried but for the last three words. That was the worst of it. Obviously, her father was working hard in the background, although he hadn't been seen in town for nearly five days. More distant ranchers and cowboys who had trusted Solomon just a short time of go had streamed in to withdraw their money. Solomon had managed not to shut his doors early once during those days, though it was a small blessing that two of those days were Saturday and Sunday, when the bank was closed anyhow. Now it was Monday morning, and the bank would open its doors once more with a much-needed Western Union delivery of cash from the sale of some of Solomon's stocks.

As much of a relief as those sales were, Honoria wasn't foolish enough to think her father wasn't already planning his next move.

She shifted to prop herself above Solomon, knees resting on either side of his hips, her honey-blonde hair falling forward to pool on the dark skin of his chest. "I've been thinking that perhaps there's something else I can do, in a small way, to help you."

Solomon grinned up at her, brushing his fingertips across her cheek. "You're already doing far more to help me than you know." He followed up his comment by smoothing his hands down her sides, pulling the sheets down with them. He cupped her backside, his fingers seeking out the part of her that was already hot and aching for him. The contrast of her body's heat and the cool air of morning kissing her skin where he'd tugged the sheet away made it difficult for her to think. She adored the way he sparked the fire within her with such bold, intimate touches.

Still, she held it together long enough to say, "I thought I might ask Wendy Montrose if I could go to work at her dress shop."

Solomon paused his ministrations, his hands covering her backside, and raised an eyebrow. His surprise softened to a smile that was as sensual as his touch. "You don't need to go to work to support me." His tone was almost laughing.

"It wouldn't *only* be for that reason," she went on, gasping as his fingers delved into the cleft between her legs, sending pleasure shooting through her. "Remember, I said I wanted to make beautiful things to be remembered by. Dresses are beautiful, and I'm quite good at making them." The words flittered out of her mind almost as soon as they were spoken as she arched her back so that she could rub her tightened nipples against his chest.

"I think we're making something beautiful right here, right now," he replied in a low rumble.

Any further argument was utterly forgotten as he lifted his hips and guided himself inside of her. Honoria was surprised by the reversal of positions—her on top, him beneath her. She caught on to the rhythm that was needed to find pleasure that way, though, and the next twenty minutes were spent lost in wild abandon.

Making love didn't solve the underlying problem, though. As Honoria and Solomon ate a hurried breakfast to make up for the time they'd lost enjoying each other's company, Solomon finally said, "If sewing for Wendy is something you honestly want to do, for your own satisfaction and not just for me, then by all means, do it."

"Really?" Honoria whirled around from where she had been putting the last of the breakfast things away and flung herself into his arms. "Oh, Solomon. No one has ever let me have my way like this before. You make me so happy."

She kissed him soundly before she could check to see if the hint about her miserable past had registered in his expression. Solomon wrapped his arms around her and indulged in the kiss. So much so that by the time he leaned back to take a breath, they were both hot and panting.

"This is not a good indicator of whether I'll be able to get the bank opened on time."

Honoria laughed at the teasing. The fact that he could tease in the midst of so much trouble lifted her spirits. "I'll go speak to Wendy right away. If she'll have me, I want to start working today. If not…"

"Any woman anywhere in this country would be honored to have you sewing for them," he said before she could go on.

She kissed him once more quickly, then spun around to rush out the door.

Wendy Montrose had come to Haskell as a mail-order bride the year before. She was intended for Cody Montrose, but as soon as Cody saw that Wendy was black—a detail Mrs. Breashears at Hurst Home in Nashville had forgotten to mention—he refused her. His brother Travis had stepped in, marrying Wendy instead, and a happier couple was hard to find. Wendy had been forced to fight against the same prejudice that Solomon was facing now to prove that she was a talented seamstress who deserved her own dress shop, but fortunately, she'd proven to the town and everyone within several counties that she was as brilliant with a needle as the finest seamstresses in Paris. Honoria should know. She was the one who had sewn most of Melinda's gowns when her angry sister had challenged Wendy to a dressmaking contest.

Wendy had her own shop on Main Street now—a shop given to her by Howard as the prize for winning the competition. The windows were filled with delectable creations—a couple of full gowns along with intricate bodices, bolts of fabric, and even a few hats she'd ordered from catalogs to sell along with her dresses. Honoria peered through the front door to see if Wendy was downstairs before knocking. Wendy had recently given birth to her and Travis's first child, a beautiful baby boy, but she was still up and moving around the shop.

"Come in," she called as Honoria knocked.

With a bright smile for the baby, Honoria swept through the front door. "How is the little treasure today?"

"Hungry as usual," Wendy laughed. She bundled the baby into Honoria's arms as she came near. "You don't have to knock, you know. Not only is my door always open to you, as I've said before, it's a place of business, not an inner sanctum."

"Old habits," Honoria explained, her voice pitching higher as tiny Emanuel Montrose blinked and snuggled into her arms. "Good morning, sweet boy," she cooed.

She reached down to tickle Emanuel, and her heart leapt in her chest as he grabbed her finger. At the same time, part of her wanted to weep. There was little chance that she would be strong enough or last long enough to give Solomon a child before she died, but if she could…

"How can I help you today? Wendy asked, blessedly allowing Honoria to push that thought aside. "Are you looking to buy a gown?"

"No," Honoria laughed. "Actually, I was coming to see if you needed help sewing."

Wendy's eyes went wide. "Do I ever! I've got more orders than I can handle, and with this little one begging for so much attention, it's all I can do to fill them in good time."

"Oh, I hoped you would say that." She laughed harder at her words. "I mean, I'm not happy that you're struggling, but now that I'm…" She stopped herself from hinting that she was dying and shifted to say instead, "Now that I'm married to Solomon and free from my family, more than anything, I want to sew for you."

"What an incredible compliment!"

Little Emanuel began to fuss, so Wendy took him back and settled him against her shoulder, rubbing his back to calm him. His skin was a shade or two lighter than Wendy's. Honoria tilted her head to the side and wondered what delicious color her and Solomon's children could have been. It gave her a sudden boost to know that they wouldn't be the only children of mixed race in Haskell.

Of course, they wouldn't *be*, but for a moment it was nice to dream.

"What a lovely smile," Wendy commented. "I have to say, Honoria, I've never seen you looking so happy and so well in all the time I've been in Haskell."

"I—" Honoria didn't know how to answer. There was no way to explain the truth. As far as she could figure, her improved appearance was just a temporary effect of having things settle into place.

"I also have to say," Wendy went on, preventing her from having to come up with some sort of awkward excuse, "that I'm ridiculously glad we've finally been able to become friends. I've been waiting almost a year for this day."

"Me too." Honoria beamed. Another wonderful side-effect of getting away from her family and marrying Solomon was that she now had more friends than she'd ever had in her life. "And since you're my friend," she rushed on, "I insist you show me what you're working on right now so that I can help."

Wendy chuckled and gestured for her to follow her to the back room. "I've just had an order for a wedding trousseau for a rancher's daughter out near Laramie. She wants everything embroidered."

The two of them shared a look of mock dread for the complicated task in front of them. In truth, Honoria couldn't have been happier. It was almost as if she wasn't sick at all and she had the world stretching out in front of her.

"...and one, two, three, four, five." Solomon finished counting the bank's cash drawer under his breath. "It's not as bad as I thought it'd be," he told Horace.

"I think that most of the major ranch owners close to Bonneville have already come in," Horace said. He touched the edge of the second box they'd set up for the account cards of men who had withdrawn their funds. What worried Solomon was that the box that held cards for open accounts was still much fuller.

He huffed an ironic laugh, shaking his head. "Give him time. Bonneville is persistent. We probably haven't seen him in town because he's out there rallying people to his cause."

Horace gave him a sympathetic look and put the account boxes and the main ledger away. "It'll all work out, boss. People will get over this fit, and when they see what a nuisance it is to take their money all the way to Everland or Rawlins, they'll be back."

"I hope you're right," Solomon sighed.

The bank's door opened, and once again, the uncomfortable pinch of worry in his gut over whether this next customer was the one who dealt the death-blow hit him. His relief was epic when he saw it was Howard and Gunn.

"Solomon!" Howard boomed as Howard did. "We've come to take you to lunch."

That pinch in his gut twisted to something entirely too sentimental. He'd always had friends, but for some reason that fact felt so much more important now. Honoria's sweetness and feeling must be rubbing off on him.

Which was just fine as far as he was concerned.

He headed to the gate and crossed into the lobby. "Normally I would turn you down. There's so much work to do. But I can't deny that I'm grateful for your presence today."

"Good." Gunn nodded. "That's as it should be."

Solomon thumped Gunn's back as he met his two friends at the door. They headed out into the hot summer day. Instead of turning left to head up to the hotel, they turned right and walked a few doors down to The Silver Dollar. The choice put a smile on Solomon's face. Sam didn't serve much in the way of food in his saloon, but he too was a good friend. At the moment, that was more important than fine dining.

"About time you three got here." Sheriff Trey Knighton was waiting with Sam at a table near the bar along with Travis Montrose and Luke Chance. The saloon didn't see a lot of business in the middle of the day, and that day was no exception. Aside from Solomon's friends, there were only a few tired vagrants snoozing in the corner. Sam habitually let men who were down on their luck take shelter in the saloon. The thought crossed Solomon's mind that as rough as Sam was, he should really find himself a good wife too. Hurst Home was still a fine option for a man looking to marry. Quite a few girls had come from there to marry ranch hands and tradesmen since Franklin Haskell started the trend.

"We saved you a seat." Travis tugged one of the chairs away from the table with the toe of his boot. He wore a confident, almost teasing smirk.

"Gentlemen." Solomon greeted the circle of his friends with a nod, but was instantly suspicious. "What's this party all about?"

Luke slapped his back as he reached the empty chair. "We figured we had a few things to discuss."

"Is that so?" Solomon sank into the chair.

The others quickly followed suit. Sam brought over a round of beers before sitting himself, making the table designed for eight feel like a boardroom. Domenica and Pearl from Bonnie's place marched out of the back room with trays of stew and fresh bread, as if the saloon was suddenly a restaurant and they were waitresses.

"No, seriously. What is going on here?" Solomon grew serious.

"We all know that you've got a heap of trouble on your hands," Trey started. "And we are all committed to making sure it goes no further than it's already gone."

A mix of gratitude and embarrassment to have caused so much disturbance sat uncomfortably in Solomon's stomach. He sipped his beer to try to dispel it.

"None of us is willing to see anyone get hurt," Travis continued. "We've been trying to keep an eye out for you in an informal way these last few days."

"So I'd noticed," Solomon drawled, arching his brow.

"We want to make it a more formal arrangement," Trey went on. "As sheriff of this town, I can't allow any of its citizens to bully any of the others, or worse."

The "or worse" was spoken almost as an afterthought, but every one of them knew it was the more important concern.

"I thank you for your concern, gentlemen," Solomon began with a wince, "but I can't ask you to go out of your way for a problem I created."

Luke snorted. "*You* didn't create any of this. Bonneville did."

"All you did was marry the girl that anyone with eyes could see you'd been longing for these last few years," Travis added.

Solomon sat straighter to fight the wave of awkwardness that rippled through him. If they only knew. "Regardless, I'm not asking you to untangle the knots I created by following my heart."

An unexpected pang hit him. Would he have broken down and pursued Honoria even if she hadn't come to him with her plight? Would he have had the courage to follow his heart without her prompting? He wasn't sure, and that devastated him. To the world, Honoria appeared meek and retiring, but she was strength personified. In just a week, she'd become the core of his strength.

What would he do without her when she was gone?

"I know that look," Trey went on with a lop-sided smirk.

No, Solomon doubted he did, but he kept his mouth shut.

"You're a proud man, Solomon, and we all admire you for it, but there comes a time when even the proudest man would do well to accept the help of his friends."

Solomon drew in a breath and crossed his arms. "What do you have in mind?"

The others shook off some of their tension and lit with enthusiasm.

"Gunn and I are here to help with the financial end of things," Howard explained.

Solomon nodded, growing more uncomfortable—and more grateful—by the second. "I managed to sell a chunk of stocks, and the proceeds have been trickling in for the last day or so."

"I've sent for some cash as well," Gunn added. "It will be there if you need it."

"We have a bit saved up too," Domenica surprised them all by speaking out in her sonorous, Spanish accent.

"I couldn't ask you to part with your hard-earned money," Solomon said with a smile. He instantly regretted calling the money hard-earned. Chances were that any money coming from Bonnie's girls was as bitterly won as possible and more.

Domenica shrugged. "I will speak to the girls." She headed back to the saloon's back room.

The men watched her go with admiration. "She always was a fine woman." Luke grinned.

Sam swatted him. "You're a married man, Luke!"

Luke's expression dropped to mock offense. "Yeah, one who never patronized Bonnie's girls in the first place, *Sam Standish*." The name was an accusation, and Sam had the good grace to blush and glance over to the other side of the room.

Trey cleared his throat and went on. "Before we start arguing over who does and doesn't spend time over at Bonnie's, I propose we set up a rotation of guards for the bank and for Solomon and Honoria's home."

The others hummed and nodded in agreement. Solomon sighed and rubbed his face. "Honoria isn't going to like it."

"No?" Howard asked.

"She's a newlywed bride." One whose health would begin to decline any day now. In fact, Solomon was surprised that with a diagnosis of consumption, she was able to breathe as deeply and make the glorious sounds she did when they were in bed. The thought pinched his brow and started him wondering.

"I bet she'd rather know you were safe than be

certain there were no ears nearby to hear," Luke said. "I know Eden would prefer I was wrapped up in cotton-wool and tucked in her pocket than worry about me getting hurt."

"True," Solomon sighed. "I still think that privacy is important to Honoria."

"And I would humbly suggest that you are *more* important," Gunn added.

It was a stirring thought, one that put a smile on Solomon's face in spite of the situation. But yet again, the pain of knowing he would lose her before they'd so much as begun a life together put a damper on the joy he so badly wanted to feel.

"What if—"

He was cut off as the saloon doors opened and none other than Rex Bonneville strode in. Not only that, he was accompanied by four men in suits that marked them as something other than rough ranch hands or hired thugs.

"Well, well." Rex sauntered up to the table, the others following. "We were told we'd find you in here. I just didn't think it would be quite such a social event."

Solomon stood to prevent Rex from towering over him as he came closer. Everyone else at the table stood as well. If it wasn't for the professional dress and demeanor of most of the men staring each other down, any outside observer would think there was about to be a shoot-out.

"Eastman, what are you doing here?" Howard barked, narrowing his eyes at one of the men standing behind Rex. "You too, Lamb."

Solomon blinked in surprise. Howard knew these men?

The one Howard had addressed as Eastman stepped forward, hooking his thumbs in the pockets of his brocade vest. "The WSGA got word that there's a bit of trouble here in Haskell. Seems some crooked darkie is trying to swindle good people out of their money." He glared at Solomon.

As the picture came clearer for Solomon, he tensed. The WSGA. They were Bonneville's trump card, and a vicious one at that.

"There is nothing of the sort going on," Howard growled in reply. "In fact, what's really going on is a case of outright bullying by a man who disagrees with the decisions his daughter has made."

One of the WSGA members glanced anxiously between Howard and Bonneville. The other three kept their gloating, petty expressions and their airs of superiority.

"We'll see about that," Eastman said.

"We're here to conduct an investigation," one of the men who hadn't shared his name yet said. He was tall and rail-thin, and had the look of a vicious schoolmaster about him.

"And who are you?" Howard snapped. "I don't know you."

"Jim O'Brien," the man said. "Special council. The WSGA hired me to audit Mr. Templesmith and his bank."

"Mr. O'Brien is here to determine if Mr. Templesmith's business is strictly aboveboard," Rex said with a smirk.

"If it's not, well, we might just have to take things into our own hands," Eastman finished.

Solomon wasn't fool enough not to know what that meant. He'd seen far too many of his black brothers swept away in the middle of the night never to be seen again, or worse, to be found in trees.

"I can assure you, sirs, that my bank is run within strict guidelines set forward by the National Banking Act of 1863," Solomon replied, summoning every bit of authority he could manage.

"We'll be the judge of that," Lamb said, eyes narrowed.

They all stood there, staring each other down, for several tense seconds. If Rex and his WSGA men were at all intimidated by the show of solidarity from the Haskell men, they didn't let on. They were, however, the first to break.

"We'll take that table over there," Rex said, heading for one of the many free tables. "And we expect a round of whiskey immediately."

Sam looked like he would mutiny and throw all five of them out, but Solomon shook his head and gestured for him to get whatever the men needed. For a few seconds, Sam still looked like he wouldn't go for it. Then he sighed, muttered under his breath, and stomped off to the bar.

"Looks like my problems just got bigger," Solomon sighed.

"Then your defense will just have to get bigger too," Gunn answered, the look in his eyes that everyone in town both admired and dreaded.

"Don't you worry." Howard thumped Solomon's back. "The WSGA fancies themselves far more powerful than they are. They don't have as much authority in Haskell as they think they do. You'll be fine."

Solomon managed to smile and nod at his friend, but he was anything but certain. Saving his business was one thing, but if Rex had brought in back-up, could he continue to protect Honoria the way she deserved?

# Chapter Ten

"Well here's a problem," Mr. O'Brien grumbled as he stood at the bank's front desk by Mr. Greeley's side.

"What problem?" Solomon glanced up from monitoring Mr. Lamb as he rifled through the contents of his desk.

Honoria sat straighter in the chair to the side of the room where she worked finishing a hem for Wendy. She was intent to keep up with the work she'd promised to do for her friend, but after Solomon explained why the men from the WSGA were there, she was loathe to leave his side.

Mr. O'Brien held up the two boxes of account cards. "You're keeping your account information in two separate places with no rhyme or reason."

Solomon's face was a mask of calm, but she knew him too well not to see the tension in his clenched jaw. "One box contains information for open accounts, and the other is for accounts that have been closed. We've been keeping them separate since—"

His explanation stopped when Mr. O'Brien turned both boxes upside down, dumping all of the cards onto the floor. Mr. Greeley yelped and dove to pick up the cards. Mr. Eastman laughed from his spot, tipped back in a chair smoking a cigar.

"Filing systems must comply with Wyoming bank regulations," Mr. O'Brien sneered before tossing the empty boxes back onto the counter.

"These were alphabetized," Mr. Greeley moaned.

"Clearly not." Mr. O'Brien had already moved on to the ledger, turning its pages roughly.

Honoria did her best to catch Solomon's attention so that she could send him a smile of support, but her dear husband was more distracted than she'd ever seen him. He rubbed his face, massaging his jaw, then rolling his shoulders. She figured it was his attempt to look nonplussed.

"This is not standard ink," Mr. Lamb said, taking a new, sealed bottle of black ink out of one of the drawers in Solomon's desk.

"I was not aware ink had standards," Solomon answered him grimly.

Mr. Lamb snorted. He glanced first to Mr. Eastman, then Mr. Chalmers. For his part, Mr. Chalmers was frowning as much as Solomon as he went over older records in a cabinet to the back of the room. The men from the WSGA had all claimed to be gentlemen and professionals, but as far as Honoria was concerned, Mr. Chalmers was the only one she would have considered applying those labels to. If only he'd speak up.

"Seems to me there are a lot of things you aren't aware of, boy," Mr. Lamb said, giving Solomon a look that Honoria wouldn't tolerate giving to a naughty child. Worse still, before any of them could react, he twisted open the bottle and upended it onto the papers strewn across Solomon's desk.

Solomon gasped and made a move to rescue the papers, but stopped before he took more than one step. It was too late. The carefully-kept records and timesheets that Mr. Lamb had scattered across the desktop were instantly ruined. Weeks, months, of work were ruined with a splash. The desktop blotter could only take so much. It was more likely than not that the mahogany desktop was stained beyond hope as well.

"I found another offense," Mr. Lamb snorted. "Improper record keeping for the last three months. That's a serious offense, *boy*."

Honoria gasped aloud. How dare the man accuse Solomon of not keeping records when everyone in the room had just witnessed him ruining them? What was even worse was that Solomon hardly blinked. He clasped his hands behind his back and stood there with fury in his eyes as if…as if he'd been treated the same way before and knew there was no point in resisting.

Just like she had spent years assuming there was no point in resisting Vivian and Melinda's bullying. These men were as bad as her sisters and worse. Vivian and Melinda treated her abominably because they thought it was their right by virtue of birth-order. The men destroying Solomon's bank in the name of protecting customers and investors had no reason to be so vicious other than the color of Solomon's skin.

And the fact that he'd had the audacity to marry a white woman.

That thought was the last straw. She stood abruptly, draping her sewing work over one arm. Her fists were clenched, and indignation burned in her eyes. Solomon pivoted to see what had prompted her to stand, and his brow flew up in surprise.

"My darling, is something wrong?"

His term of endearment left the WSGA men gaping. Mr. Eastman recovered enough to spit tobacco from his cigar on Solomon's clean floor.

"I can't stand by and let this continue," Honoria managed to seethe.

Solomon let his arms drop to his sides and rushed across the room to her. "There's nothing you can do to stop it without making the situation worse. Trust me."

She stared up into his eyes, holding his gaze. She trusted him with her life. What she didn't trust was the malice of bullies and brutes. "I will stop this," she said, barely above a whisper but as certainly as if she held all the power in the world in her hands.

"I'd rather you didn't interact with these men," Solomon said, leaning closer and speaking even softer.

Honoria shook her head, drawing in a deep breath. "I don't need to speak to *them* to stop it." Solomon frowned in confusion, but she went on. "I'll be back later this afternoon."

Without waiting for him to question what she meant or where she was going, she hugged the dress she'd been sewing tighter and marched for the gate in the counter and on to the lobby door.

"I keep asking myself what a pretty little piece like you would be up for without this monkey around to defile you," Mr. Eastman called after her.

"I'll thank you not to make comments like that about my wife," Solomon growled in reply.

"You want to try to stop me?" Mr. Eastman challenged him.

Honoria had reached the door, but she turned back, catching Mr. Greeley's eyes. "Do *not* let them get into a fight," she whispered.

"I'll do my best, ma'am." Mr. Greeley shrugged.

Leaving was excruciatingly painful, but she had to do it. As soon as the bank door shut behind her, Honoria dashed down the street to Wendy's shop. She barely had time to return the dress and ask if Travis had any horses at the livery that she could borrow before she was moving on to have him saddle one of those horses. She hadn't done much riding in her day, but she had been raised on a ranch. She knew enough to hook her knee around the sidesaddle and to nudge the horse into a run.

The ride out to her father's ranch passed in a blur as her mind swirled around and around over what she could do or say once she got there. It was a huge risk to ride back into the lion's den after making her escape, but she couldn't let things continue on the way they were going.

It was a piece of luck that the entire family and Bonnie were sitting out at the table on the porch enjoying their lunch as she rode up.

"Oh my heavens, is that Honoria?" Bebe half stood out of her chair, raising a hand to shield her eyes.

By the time Honoria reached the side of the house, Bebe wasn't the only one standing. Her father and Bonnie had gotten up too. Only Melinda, Vivian, and Rance continued eating as though nothing were out of the ordinary.

"It's about time you came to your senses and returned to your family." Rex greeted her with a victorious sneer.

Honoria struggled down from her borrowed horse and glared at him. "I have not come to my senses." It wasn't what she had planned to say, but she was damned if she was going to take back a single word that came out of her mouth where her father was concerned.

"Then why are you here?" Rex's smugness melted to suspicion.

"Come have lunch with us," Bebe asked, a hint of desperation in her voice.

"Who are you to issue invitations, you ignorant twit?" Melinda snapped.

"She's an idiot," Vivian followed, though not as enthusiastically as Honoria would have expected. "You can't expect anything sensible to come out of her mouth."

"But I was just asking if Honoria—"

"Shut up, Bebe!" Melinda and Vivian rounded on their sister simultaneously.

Honoria felt sick to her stomach as her suspicions about the way Vivian and Melinda were now treating Bebe seemed to be proven. It wasn't long until she had other things to feel sick about.

"You sure are fetching when you're riled up, Viv," Cousin Rance snorted. "Gets me all hot and bothered."

"Don't you dare touch me, Rance Bonneville!" Vivian snapped with such ferocity and with a hard jerk to the side. Honoria didn't need to see it to know Rance had groped her under the table.

Honoria had taken advantage of the distraction to tie her horse to the porch railing and to ascend the stairs to face her father. "I want you to tell those men from the WSGA to stop tormenting my husband and to go back to wherever it is they came from." She was shocked at the strength of her demand, but not shocked enough to back away from it.

For a moment, her father looked like he didn't know what to make of it either. All too quickly, his brittle grin returned. "Leave them alone to do their work. You don't understand it anyhow. You don't understand what's in your own best interests."

"Don't I?" Her voice rose an octave. "I understand what's right for me far better than you do. I demand you stop this at once." She clenched her hands into fists at her sides, certain from the heat that infused her that she was red with fury.

"Honoria." Bonnie stepped forward, hands held out cautiously to her. "Are you quite certain this is the best way to approach things? You're in such a delicate condition as it is."

"Did that n— knock her up?" Rance blurted.

The edges of Honoria's vision blackened with shock and fury. Melinda yelped in offense. Vivian burst into tears and hid her face in her hands.

"So help me, God," Rex seethed, "if that mongrel has spoiled you with his seed, I will personally see him hung by his entrails."

There was no way for any of them to know that pregnancy was the furthest thing from Honoria's mind or capabilities, but it only proved what her father was capable of. "I would view any child of Solomon's growing within me as a miracle and a blessing. If you're so small-minded that you would destroy an entire family because it doesn't fit your profile, then perhaps you shouldn't consider me a part of your family at all anymore."

"How dare you?" Rex stepped closer, towering over her and raising a hand.

"Rex!" Bonnie rushed forward to grab his fist before he could land any blow. Rex shook her off violently. If not for the nearby porch rail, Bonnie would have spilled to the ground.

"Wow!" Rance called from the table. "I guess if I wanted some fight in my filly, I married the wrong sister."

Oddly, his boorish comment deflated some of the dangerous tension on the porch.

"You can have him," Vivian wailed. "He's nothing but a vulgar, overbearing, foul, heathen who can't keep his hands—" She snapped her lips closed and hid her face in her napkin.

"Aw, come on, Vivs." Rance guffawed. "I thought you liked it when I got all handsy with you." He winked, and in a shockingly bold move, closed a hand around one of her breasts and made a sound like a horn.

Vivian burst into a sobbing scream and pushed her chair back. She leapt up from the table and lunged toward Rex. "Why did you make me marry him, why? He's nothing but a loud brute!"

"He's a Bonneville, and since I have no sons—" He glared at Bonnie. "—he's the closest thing I have to an heir. He will learn how to manage this ranch, and the two of you and your children will inherit it when I'm gone."

"I don't want to inherit the ranch!" Vivian wailed. "I don't want to have his children. Give it to someone else. Give it to her!"

Honoria's eyes popped wide as Vivian flung a pointed finger in her direction. Vivian then proceeded to wilt with tears, so much so that she would have collapsed if Melinda hadn't jumped up to catch her.

"Well, I for one am never marrying," Melinda declared. "I'm not ever going to let a man touch me the way that animal…" She let her proclamation drop as Vivian redoubled her crying.

Up until that moment, Honoria was ready to rush to Vivian's aid, no matter how horrible she'd been over the years. It was unbearable to think that her sister was being used and abused by a garish husband and a callous father. But something in the overabundance of Vivian's tears, something in the suspicious way Bonnie pressed her lips together and Bebe rolled her eyes, told Honoria that there was more act than truth to Vivian's hysterics. Was it possible life with Rance wasn't as bad as she made it out to be, and that she was only carrying on to suck in all the sympathy she could?

"Not one of you is as useful to me as a son!" Rex bellowed, throwing up his hands.

"Hey!" Rance finally stood, still chewing a bite of roast as he did. "I thought you said I was just as good as a son now. I'm learnin' the whole ranching business, ain't I?"

Rex sighed heavily and wiped his hand across his red and sweating face. "If you don't run the place into the ground first." Honoria was certain he hadn't meant to issue his complaint loud enough for her to hear, but hear she did.

Hear and absorb.

Something clicked in her chest. Something that felt very much like leverage.

"I demand that you call off your dogs where Solomon is concerned." She tried her ultimatum again. "He's the greatest ally you could possibly look to in your future."

"What?" Rex snapped, scowling at her.

Honoria laughed humorlessly. "By your own admission, the ranch is in trouble. Your precious ranch that you've always loved more than any of us, more than mother."

The fact that Rex didn't dispute the accusation, but only stood there looking peevish was enough to prove it.

"Bringing in a cousin to marry Vivian and take over was a horrible mistake, and I think you know it," Honoria rushed on. "In spite of your meddling, Solomon will rise above the mess you've thrown him in. Someday when I'm gone, he'll be the only person you can turn to."

"When you're gone?" Rex paled.

"I'll be dead before you know it."

She clamped her mouth shut, certain she would be blushing furiously if she wasn't already red from anger. She hadn't come out here to tell her family she was dying. The last thing she wanted was for them to get a single hint of her illness. They would think it made her weak, able to be manipulated.

But to her great surprise, her father stepped forward and grasped her arms. "What have they done to you? What have they threatened you with?"

For the first time in the confrontation, Honoria wanted to shrink back. Rex held her firmly in place, though, an inexplicable panic in his eyes. "I—"

"I told them they were not to hurt you, only him. They weren't to harass you or lay a single finger on you. You're *my* daughter!"

Any temptation to think that her father wanted her spared out of love was dashed by those last words. No, he just didn't want his property damaged. But his outburst proved what she'd suspected all along.

"Those men are harassing my husband under your orders." It was a statement, not a question. She knew the truth, and she could see her father for everything he was now.

"I told them not to hurt you." He let go and took a hard step back.

"Then tell them not to hurt Solomon either." Her mind raced. There was no guarantee her father would do a single thing she said. The only thing she could bargain with was his own sense of pride and self-importance. "I swear to God above, Papa, if any of those men lays a finger on Solomon, I will go down with him, fighting all the way." Death would come for her sooner than later, so why not use it to her advantage? "And everyone will know you were behind it."

Rex took another step away from her. The blood drained from his face. He wiped his hand over his mouth as though trying to wash away a sour taste. And that was how she knew she had him. She wasn't proud of the way she'd won, but she'd won nonetheless.

"I'll tell them to use no physical force," he conceded at last, voice hoarse with frustration. "I cannot and will not stop them from completing their investigation."

"They will find nothing wrong with the way my husband conducts business," Honoria promised him. "You will come out of this looking like a raving, jealous fool."

"How dare you speak to Papa that way?" Melinda yelped.

"Does no one care about my poor, wretched nerves?" Vivian wailed.

"Papa does kind of look bad in this," Bebe added quietly.

"Shut up, Bebe!" Melinda and Vivian barked at her.

"Come on." Bonnie rushed forward, wedging herself between Honoria and Rex, and taking Honoria's arm. "I'll help you mount up so you can go home to your husband."

Honoria was still so caught up in the power and awe of everything she'd said and done that she let Bonnie lead her off the porch without protest. Honoria wasn't sure she'd ever seen Bonnie so tense, though.

"Consumption, eh?" she murmured as they reached the spot where Travis's spare horse was tied.

"What?" Honoria shook herself out of her emotions.

"Isn't consumption supposed to waste you away? Make you weak?"

Honoria blinked at Bonnie.

"Are you coughing up much blood?"

"I…" Honoria pressed a hand to her chest, feeling that she should probably be breaking down into a coughing fit right then and there. But she wasn't. Her lungs didn't even feel tight. "I haven't coughed blood. I suppose I haven't reached that stage of the disease yet."

"Bonnie! Get back up here!" Rex shouted, recovering himself.

Bonnie sent a wary look over her shoulder. She bent down to form a cradle for Honoria to put her foot in, then hoisted her up into the saddle. "You run home to your husband as quick as you can and tell him what Rex just said. Maybe it'll help."

Honoria nodded, gathering the reins. "Bonnie," she added before she turned the horse to spur him on. "You be careful."

Bonnie looked up at her with a sad smile. "Honey, I've been doing this longer than you can imagine. I know how to be careful around men who have foul tempers."

Something about the comment ignited far more questions than it answered. There was a story there, a story Bonnie wasn't telling. Honoria would give anything to know what it was, but now was not the time. Bonnie was right, Solomon needed her. She nudged the horse to turn toward the drive, then set off at a run for home.

# Chapter Eleven

Breakfast was unusually quiet. Solomon sighed over yet another confirmation of sale of stock, then set the telegram on the pile beside his plate. He reached for his coffee, glancing across to Honoria as he took a gulp. As beautiful as ever, Honoria was unusually quiet. She picked at her scrambled eggs with the edge of her fork, but Solomon didn't think she was seeing her food.

"Is everything all right, sweetheart?" he asked. It was one thing to be concerned for his business, but concern for his wife opened up places in his heart that he hadn't known existed. "Honoria?"

"Hmm?" She popped out of her thoughts, lifting her brow as she met his eye. She shook her head. "Oh. I'm just worried about everything going on."

Solomon sent her what he hoped was a reassuring smile. "Don't let it worry you too much. The whole point of the two of us being together is so that you can have peace and happiness, not strain and strife while…" He let the rest go. There was no reason to upset her—or himself—by reminding them that as close as they were to the beginning, everything would soon come to an end.

Honoria did her best to smile in return. "I'm less worried than I was."

Solomon wasn't sure what to say to that, so he took another gulp of coffee. Honoria had run off in a fury the other day, when the men from the WSGA were vandalizing his bank in the name of their investigation. She'd made no secret of the fact that she'd been out to her father's ranch and had had words with him, but instinct told him there was something more.

"Luke was telling me last night that he hasn't seen a single suspicious person loitering near the house or the bank for the past few days," he told Honoria, hoping that bit of information would prove that whatever she'd said to her father had been effective.

"I'm glad." She smiled, but her gaze was fixed on her plate—or rather on the white handkerchief next to her plate—once more.

Solomon frowned. He set his coffee aside and went about finishing his breakfast. What had Honoria so…distracted? She wasn't upset like she'd been the other day at the bank. There was something more, as if she was working out a puzzle in her head. Strangely, he thought her handkerchief had something to do with it.

A terrible thought hit him. He swallowed and made himself ask, "Are you feeling well?" She'd been so energetic and fiery since their wedding day—at night especially—but it would do him no good to pretend that this fit of melancholy wasn't related to her illness. What if she was beginning to feel poorly at last?

She took too long to reply. In fact, she only looked up at him when the silence between them went on long enough for her to realize he'd asked her a question.

"Fine, fine," she answered, then frowned, more puzzled than ever.

Solomon chewed a bite of bacon. "Maybe as soon as this foolish investigation into my bank is over we should take a vacation. I hear the seaside is good for those suffering from...lung problems." He couldn't bring himself to call her illness what it was. Consumption had too much finality to it.

Honoria sent him a sad, wary look. "It might be difficult for us to travel anywhere outside of Haskell. There aren't many other places I can think of where we would be accepted as married."

He hated that. He should have considered it before agreeing to marry her. It was the reason he had held off speaking his heart to her for so long in the first place. But instead of addressing the bitter issue directly, he feigned resignation and tapped the pile of telegrams beside his place. "There's a fair chance we don't actually have the money to go away either."

"Is there?" She seemed to focus more, her expression deeply concerned for him.

Solomon shrugged. "I've had to liquidate more than half of my investments to meet the demands of the ranchers and local workers who keep coming in insisting on withdrawing their money. There have been three Western Union deliveries already. That leaves less and less in terms of profits that I can call my own...our own."

"But the flood of people coming in has to stop eventually," Honoria reasoned. "My father's reach isn't that long."

"It only has to be long enough to—"

He was interrupted by a loud knock on the front door. Both Solomon and Honoria jerked straight in their chairs and turned to the hall. A second knock sounded.

Solomon glanced to Honoria, then stood and strode into the hall.

One of the porters from Gunn's hotel waited on his front porch.

"Can I help you?" Solomon asked as Honoria came up behind him to see what the fuss was.

The porter swallowed. "Sorry, sir. Mr. Eastman wanted me to hand-deliver this to you."

Solomon's heart sank as the porter handed a simple scrap of folded paper to him. He nodded to the young man, who nodded in return, then headed on his way. Solomon turned back into the house, unfolding the paper to read.

"What does it say?" Honoria asked as she shut the door.

Solomon sighed. "The WSGA contingent has finished their investigation. They're demanding my presence at the hotel immediately to hear what they've determined."

Honoria wrung her hands, looking pale. Her expression betrayed that she had no more confidence that the WSGA men would to come to a fair conclusion than he had. "What do we do?"

"We go to the hotel and hear what they have to say," Solomon answered. "It's the only thing we can do."

A sort of resigned calm came over Honoria. She smoothed her hands on her skirt, then said, "Then we'd better clean up breakfast and get over there."

The two of them worked in tandem to clean up the dishes and leftovers from breakfast as fast as possible. Solomon finished his coffee as he worked, figuring he would probably need it. Once everything at their house was in order, he took Honoria's arm and escorted her out to Station Street and up to the hotel.

It was a possible stroke of luck that they crossed

paths with Howard as they reached the top of Main Street.

"Good morning, Mr. Templesmith, Mrs. Templesmith." Howard greeted them with all his usual bombast. His wide smile faltered as soon as he saw the serious expressions both Solomon and Honoria wore. "What is it?"

"The WSGA have completed their investigation," Solomon answered, strangely glad to have someone to tell. "I've been summoned like some medieval serf to hear their conclusions."

Howard's frown darkened. "I'm coming with you."

A small part of Solomon thought he should argue, that he should face this firing squad alone, but Howard had as much right to hear what these interlopers had to say about the bank in his town as anyone.

The hotel was its usual calm, orderly self when they crossed the threshold into the lobby. Gunn was waiting for them and came out from behind the front desk to meet them in the middle of the room.

"They demanded I set them up in one of the private parlors as if this was some kind of inquisition," he grumbled. "I would have ignored their request but for the fact that I assumed you'd want to deal with this in private."

"Thank you, Gunn." Solomon nodded to the man, his other staunchest ally. "We already know that whatever they say is going to be bad, so it might as well be said where other ears can't hear it. Show me the way."

Gunn held out his arm, gesturing to one of the side halls off of the lobby. Solomon exchanged another look with Honoria before following him. It was strange to him how he had always prided himself on being stalwart and immovable on his own, but in the scant two weeks since Honoria had been by his side, he felt immeasurably stronger. He would give up his entire banking business and every cent he had if he could only keep her by his side forever.

Gunn stopped in front of a door at the far end of the hall and knocked to announce their presence, then opened the door. As he did, Solomon shifted so that he held Honoria's hand instead of escorting her.

"They're here," Gunn said, preceding them into the room.

"They?" Lamb blurted just as Solomon and Honoria stepped in.

The four WSGA men had set themselves up at a long table at one end of the room, like judges on a bench. They had been smoking long enough to make the air in the room thick. Solomon was instantly more concerned for Honoria's lungs than anything else, but she seemed to take it in good stride. Where judges would have stacks of books on the table to back up their findings, the only thing on the WSGA table—besides Eastman's feet—was a single piece of paper in front of O'Brien. The whole thing instantly put Solomon on edge.

But before he could say anything or demand the men share their results then leave, Howard barreled into the room.

"What nonsense are you blackguards up to now?" he demanded.

Solomon thought about letting Howard know it was all right, he didn't need to start a war on his behalf, but the shocked looks on the WSGA men's faces kept his mouth shut. He settled into a comfortable stance, squeezing Honoria's hand and wondering what Howard would do next.

"This is a private meeting," Eastman said, dropping his feet from the table and sitting up straighter.

"This is a witch-hunt," Howard corrected him.

"It is a sanctioned investigation by the Wyoming Stock Growers Association that has been initiated based on the evidence of one of its foremost members." O'Brien sniffed with all the arrogance of a bean-counting bureaucrat.

"Foremost members?" Howard boomed. "Rex Bonneville is nothing more than an ass. No, he's the pimple on a particularly round ass." Solomon nearly choked, especially when Howard flinched and turned to Honoria to say, "Terribly sorry, Mrs. Templesmith."

"No, no." Honoria couldn't hide her grin. "At the moment, I'm forced to agree that that's an apt description of my father."

"You should be grateful that your father is trying to get you out of the shameful position you've landed yourself in, young lady," Lamb snapped.

"I beg your pardon?" Howard roared.

Honoria held up a hand. It was a simple gesture, but Howard looked chastised and took a step back.

"My father does not understand my decision nor the position I am in," she said, facing the men behind the table boldly. Solomon's chest swelled with pride.

"Poppycock." Lamb snorted. "It's a disgrace to see a woman like you debasing yourself for a man like him."

"Because I am white and he is black?" Honoria raised her voice. When none of the men answered immediately, she went on with, "This is not 1850, gentlemen. Men of color are no longer enslaved. It's 1876, the centennial of a nation founded on ideals of liberty and equality, and it's high time you realize that a man's appearance or birth are no indication of his character or their ability to excel in life."

"Here, here!" Howard cheered her.

"Radical nonsense!" Lamb shouted.

"Blasphemy!" Eastman agreed. "Though we should expect no better coming from the feeble mind of a woman." He leaned across the table, narrowing his eyes at Honoria. "They never should have given you people the vote in this state. Mark my words, we'll fix that mistake in a few years! If this isn't raw evidence of your inability to think and your rash and imbecilic temperament, then I don't know what is. You need a *real* husband to take you in hand and beat this impertinence out of you."

"I revise my opinion, gentlemen." O'Brien tilted his nose up as if both Honoria and Solomon stank. "These two...*things* deserve each other."

An odd mix of emotion pounded through Solomon. On the one hand, he could have beat all three men into a bloody pulp for insulting Honoria. On the other, he couldn't have agreed with them more. He and Honoria were meant to be together. They were a matched set, a perfect union.

And when she died she would take a part of him with her.

The fourth man at the table, Chalmers, who had so far sat there looking increasingly embarrassed, cleared his throat. "Gentlemen, perhaps we should get to our findings and conclude this interview as quickly as possible."

The other three sneered at him but settled into their chairs. Solomon nodded shortly to Chalmers in thanks, but Chalmers refused to look at him. The man wasn't an enemy, but like far too many others, he wasn't going to lift a finger to help if it put him in a bad position with the bigger bullies in the schoolyard.

O'Brien picked up the paper in front of him and read, "It is the conclusion of the investigating committee of the Wyoming Stock Growers Association that Mr. Solomon

Templesmith is in violation of several banking standards, as laid out by the National Banking Act of 1863, including failure to keep adequate records, failure to comply with solubility standards, and failure to provide the necessary information to the investigating authorities."

"Solomon provided every one of those things to you," Honoria protested. "*You* were the ones who destroyed and mangled his records, and as to your solubility standards—"

Solomon squeezed Honoria's hand, prompting her to take a breath instead of railing on. He could have shouted and raged enough to bring the hotel down around them at the unfairness of it all, but experience had taught him it would do no good. There was nothing he could do to stop the tide from coming in, but if he was clever, he could make himself a boat to get over and past it.

O'Brien stared down his nose at Honoria and her interruption as though she was a swollen tick he'd found on a dog. He cleared his throat and went on. "Therefore, this committee has determined that if sufficient funds are not provided for any and every customer wishing to withdraw their funds from this sub-par institution, legal action shall be taken."

"Though we won't necessarily have to get the law involved in meting out punishment," Eastman added in an ominous growl.

"This is outrageous," Howard bellowed. "I will not have you threatening citizens of my town."

"Also," O'Brien added before the others could get into any sort of confrontation with Howard, "the WSGA is imposing a fine on Mr. Templesmith in the amount of five thousand dollars." He set the paper down with a smug grin. "Payable immediately."

"What?" Howard gasped.

Solomon clenched his jaw, fighting with everything he had not to give the men behind the table the reaction they wanted. It would only make things worse if he lost his temper, justifiably or not. At least the materials he needed for that boat he'd use to rise above the tide were there. Enough money to cover the ridiculous fine would be arriving on the train that morning.

"Is that all?" he asked, his voice low and dark.

The WSGA men lost some of their swagger. They exchanged looks with each other. Eastman and Lamb looked furious that they hadn't gotten to lash out and put Solomon down the way they had Honoria. Chalmers refused to look at the others, appearing as though he might be sick. Only O'Brien maintained a poker face as stony as Solomon's. "That's all," he said.

Solomon nodded. "I'll go get your money." He turned to go, resting a hand on Honoria's back to bring her with him. These men may have won the battle, but they wouldn't win the war.

Honoria was beside herself with grief and frustration by the time she and Solomon, Howard and Mr. Gunn, made it back to the lobby. She understood and admired Solomon's stoic way of handling the situation, but the whole thing was so wrong, so infuriating, to begin with. And to impose such a mind-boggling fine? She was certain they had made it up solely to break Solomon.

"I can scrape together a little extra cash from my holdings in Ohio and Pennsylvania," Howard said as soon as they were in a quiet corner of the lobby.

"You're always welcome to borrow from me," Gunn added. "Although I'll have to liquidate a few more assets to provide enough for the fine."

"No." Solomon shook his head. "I have cash coming

via Western Union on today's train. It will be enough."

Honoria practically shook with fury over it all. Fury led to a coughing fit the likes of which she hadn't had in days. A coughing fit that squeezed her lungs but didn't produce a single fleck of blood. She frowned.

"Mrs. Templesmith, would you like a glass of water?" Gunn asked, ever considerate.

His tiny offer of kindness broke some of the tension in Honoria's soul. "Yes, please."

Gunn smiled. "Here." He offered Honoria his arm.

Honoria sent Solomon a weary smile, then took Gunn's arm and walked across the lobby with him as Solomon and Howard continued their conversation with Solomon saying, "This is going to severely drain my assets."

Honoria squeezed her eyes shut for a second, trusting Gunn to guide her. This was her fault. Like it or not, as beautiful as everything else was, none of this would be happening to Solomon if it wasn't for her, if it wasn't for her illness. He was suffering for her.

"I'm certain you will both weather this storm." Gunn shook her out of her thoughts as they reached the door to the restaurant. He waved for one of the wait staff to bring a glass of water. "Solomon is as tough as he is refined."

"Yes, and I am an albatross around his neck," Honoria sighed.

"Don't say that." Gunn turned to face her, holding on to her hands. "You're a remarkable young lady who has given him a reason to fight."

She couldn't help but smile weakly. "You're kind to say so, Mr. Gunn, but at the end of the day, I don't want to be the cause of his ruin. None of this would be happening if not for me."

The waiter brought a clear glass of water to Gunn,

who handed it to Honoria, then nodded for the worker to give them some space. Honoria was surprised by how refreshing a simple glass of cold water was right then. She was surprised that it didn't send her into a another coughing fit, that the entire sorry meeting hadn't doubled her over. Or perhaps it would have been more accurate to say that it made her suspicious.

For the last few days, she hadn't been able to get one tiny thing Bonnie had said to her as she was leaving her father's ranch out of her head. Consumptives were supposed to cough blood. Not once, not even when her attacks had been at their worst, had she seen so much as a speck of blood. On top of that, she couldn't remember ever feeling as whole and healthy—at least physically—in the last two weeks. She needed to find out if Dr. Meyers had returned from his business with the Cheyenne and ask for more details about the usual progress of her disease.

Gunn waited until she had refreshed herself before taking the glass from her, setting it on a side table, and going on with, "This is hardly your fault, Honoria. Ignorant, spiteful men don't need much to use as an excuse to attack the people they despise on principle. There are many who have resented Solomon's success for years now."

"But they chose to attack him because of me," she argued.

Gunn shook his head. "If it wasn't you, it would have been something else. And you bring Solomon so much joy."

She arched a brow and took his arm when he offered to escort her back to where Solomon and Howard still had their heads together in discussion. "Do I?"

"Absolutely," Gunn nearly laughed.

"I know I bring him some happiness." She blushed at

the thought of exactly what form that happiness took. "I just don't know if that's enough to make up for the misery I've caused." Misery that could only double when her strange health eventually did take the downturn that was in store.

They reached Solomon and Howard just as Solomon was muttering, "I'm just glad that, because of her illness, Honoria won't be around to see my life in shambles."

It felt as though a sharp arrow struck Honoria's heart. Even when Solomon whipped to face her and said, "Sweetheart, I'm so sorry. That's not how I meant that at all." He broke away from Howard and swept her out of Gunn's grasp and into his arms. "I'm so sorry."

Honoria managed a weak smile. "No, I understand completely." She did, but that didn't mean the entire situation didn't hurt. "I only wish that I could be there with you to face whatever is coming. It's my fault that it's coming in the first place."

"Don't let yourself think that," he said, then followed it up with a kiss. That kiss went farther to set her at ease than anything else he could have said. "I made a promise to you, and it's a promise I intend to keep."

Somehow, Honoria's heart felt light while the world weighed down on her shoulders. She embraced Solomon, leaning her head against his shoulder. His arms felt so right as they closed around her, as if he could protect her from the storm. But she never should have asked him for that protection in the first place.

In the distance, a train whistle sounded. Solomon squeezed her tighter for a moment, then let her go and stood back. "That's the train with my money on it," he sighed. "Might as well go pick it up so I can hand it over to your buddies." He glanced to Howard.

"I may be a member of the WSGA," Howard growled, "but they are *not* my buddies."

"All the same..."

They started for the door, waving goodbye to Gunn. Howard parted ways with them at the bottom of the porch stairs. Honoria walked on for a few paces at Solomon's side before pausing.

"I need to run an errand before I head over to Wendy's for work," she said.

Solomon looked confused for a moment before his features softened. "Do you need any help?"

"No." She shook her head. "I've imposed on you far too much already."

"Darling, you really haven't." He leaned in to kiss her. "I married you because I wanted to."

She wanted to argue with him so desperately, but just like arguing with the WSGA men wouldn't do him any good, so arguing that all of their troubles were her fault would get her nowhere.

"Those men don't know a true hero when they see one," she said instead, fighting to keep the tears out of her voice.

"Or a true heroine," he added.

He kissed her once more, said a few tender words of goodbye, then headed on to Main Street. Honoria clutched a hand to her heart for a moment, watching him go, before turning and hurrying down Prairie Avenue. She needed to know how much longer she could hold on. She needed to find Dr. Meyers and ask him if she would be gone and out of Solomon's life soon. As bitter a pill to swallow as it was, the sooner she found her eternal rest, the easier it would be for Solomon to move on without being harassed.

She nearly wept in relief when she saw the shingle out in front of the Meyers house proclaiming that Dr.

Meyers had returned from his Cheyenne business. His office was around the back of the house with its own private entrance. The day was balmy and breezy, so he had all of his windows as well as the front door opened. Honoria dashed through the door, ready to learn the truth and get it over with. Dr. Meyers's nurse, Abigail, lifted her head from the desk where she was going through piles of patient files.

"Oh, Miss Honoria!" Abigail gasped. "I'm so glad you came in."

"Is Dr. Meyers here?" Honoria didn't bother to correct Abigail's use of her old form of address.

"He is, and he's desperate to see you."

Honoria frowned as Abigail jumped up from her desk. Before Abigail could even make it to the door to the examination room, Dr. Meyers poked his head around the corner.

"Honoria! You have no idea how glad I am to see you. Come in, come in." There was something strained and worried in his expression as he stepped aside and invited her into the examination room.

Her heart in her throat, Honoria slipped past him and into the tiny room. Her entire day—the last two weeks, really—had been so out of the ordinary that she didn't know if the roiling in her stomach was nerves or illness. She needed answers, though, and if she could stand up to a table full of men intent on destroying her husband, she could face the truth of her death.

"Dr. Meyers, I need to know how long—"

"I've been desperate to ride out to your father's ranch to apologize," he spoke at the same time as her.

Something snapped inside her with a foreboding crack. "A-apologize?"

"Yes." Dr. Meyers winced. "If I had known what Dr.

Abernathy would do, I would have made a point of finding you to tell you the results of your tests before leaving for the Cheyenne camp."

"That wasn't necessary." Honoria began to feel dizzy. "Dr. Abernathy gave me the results."

"But that's just it," Dr. Meyers said, looking downright stricken. "He mixed up the files. He gave you the wrong results. Mrs. Bonita, who was in town to visit her nephew, has consumption. You're just fine. There's nothing wrong with you at all."

# *Chapter Twelve*

Thank God there was a chair in Dr. Meyers's examination room. Honoria sat down hard as her knees gave out. Her mind couldn't comprehend what Dr. Meyers had told her. It was as if everything stopped—her brain, her heart, her breathing. She could only gape at nothing, in total shock.

"Your symptoms were most likely caused by stress," Dr. Meyers went on, shifting anxiously from one foot to the other. "I know that your situation at home is often difficult, and I believe that your loss of energy and coughing is a result of mental and emotional fatigue. If there was some way that you could get away from your family, if only for holidays, separate yourself from the cause, as it were…"

His words drifted off. He tilted his head to the side and regarded Honoria with concern and more than a little guilt.

"I really am terribly sorry about the mix-up. Dr. Abernathy should have looked at those files more closely. I…I hope this hasn't caused you any undue trouble."

At last, Honoria dragged her eyes up to meet Dr. Meyers's. "I married Solomon." The words escaped from her in a daze before she could stop herself.

"Solomon Templesmith?" Dr. Meyers's face brightened. "That's wonderful! I've noticed that the two of you have always seemed fond of one another." He paused, letting out a relieved breath, and burst into a smile. "This is delightful. Exactly what you need for your health. And let me guess, since the wedding you've been feeling hale and healthy and have been experiencing fewer symptoms?"

Honoria blinked and lowered her head. She *was* feeling better. She hadn't been coughing nearly as much, not at all some days. In her heart of hearts, she'd known that being with Solomon was good for her on a hundred different levels. She should have known the truth, that she wasn't dying at all.

*She wasn't dying.*

"I married Solomon under false pretenses," she squeaked.

The reality of the situation she was in—the situation she'd put Solomon in—crashed down around her like a house crumbling. She shot to her feet so fast it made her dizzy and clutched her stomach. She'd manipulated a good man into marrying her for selfish reasons, and now those reasons didn't exist. She'd brought a heap of trouble down on Solomon's head for no good reason. He was on the verge of losing everything because of her, because of some gallant idea that he could be a comfort to her in the last days of her life. But these weren't the last days of her life. She could live for fifty years more, and he'd shackled himself to her and all the problems that came with her.

"He'll never forgive me," she whispered.

Dr. Meyers reached out to steady her. "I'm sorry, I

don't understand. Won't Solomon be overjoyed by this news?"

Honoria shook her head, tears stinging at her eyes. "He only married me because I told him I was dying."

"Oh." Dr. Meyers frowned…but it was more of a frown as if something didn't quite add up. "It has to be more than that, though. I've known Solomon for quite some time, and he has always had a warm spot in his heart for you."

She swallowed the urge to be sick and stepped back from him. "My father has attacked him for marrying me. He's trying to ruin the bank because of me. Solomon is about to lose everything. It's all my fault."

Dr. Meyers let out a sympathetic breath and rubbed a hand over his face. "I'm sure he won't see it that way."

But Honoria had a terrible, terrible feeling he would. Everything was always her fault somehow. Hadn't Vivian and Melinda been telling her that for years? She'd fought and fought against their bullying, but now she was seeing it in another light. What if they were right? What if she was every bit as stupid and ham-fisted as they'd always told her she was? She'd certainly mangled her own life, and she'd managed to bring down a good man in the process.

Without waiting for another word from Dr. Meyers, she turned and fled the clinic. She wasn't sure where she would go—just like the day she'd been given the news that she was dying. She could hardly think beyond repeating "I lied to Solomon. I lied to him about the most important thing ever. I'm a liar" over and over.

Her mother's dying words began to loop over her own. "Your honor is your shining light… Be honest in all things." She'd failed her mother as certainly as she'd failed Solomon.

But she hadn't known, that gentle voice in her whispered. Surely it couldn't be a lie if she hadn't known the truth.

She ran on, turning onto Station Street and hurrying past the intersection with Main Street.

"Honoria? There you are."

Her head whipped up as Wendy called her name. Honoria stopped running, but her heart continued to thunder in her chest, and she couldn't catch her breath. Wendy was standing on the boardwalk in front of her shop, bouncing Emanuel in her arms, but started down the walk toward Honoria. As desperately as Honoria wanted to run, her feet were suddenly glued to the spot. The sudden truth would affect her friends too. She'd deceived Wendy, deceived all of the people who had come forward to be her friends, even if she hadn't told any of them she was dying.

"Are you all right?" Wendy's expression flashed to concern as she came near. "You look as though you've seen a ghost."

For some reason, Honoria laughed aloud, though the sound wasn't joyful. Up until just a few minutes ago, she'd thought she *was* the ghost.

"Here." Wendy put on a smile and attempted to hand Emanuel over to her.

Honoria stepped back, refusing Emanuel and shaking her head. "I can't. It…it wouldn't be right." Not until she found a way to make up for the magnitude of her deception.

Emanuel fussed as if indignant that "Auntie Honoria" wouldn't hold him. Wendy hugged him close, continuing to study Honoria with a troubled look.

"Something is wrong. I can see that much. Won't you tell me what it is?" Wendy asked.

Honoria swallowed, wringing her hands. Part of her wanted to confess. The rest of her wanted to hide. "I've done something terrible," she said. "Terrible and unfair. Solomon is on the verge of losing everything, and it's all my fault."

"Oh, now, I'm sure it's not—"

She couldn't stand to hear one more person say it wasn't her fault when she knew that beyond a shadow of a doubt it was. Shaking her head, she turned and ran on, desperate to get home.

But where was her home? Every fiber of her being wanted Solomon's house to be her home. She had never been happier in her life than she had under his roof, under his care and protection. But she'd obtained that care under false pretenses, and look what it had done.

No, her true home was the same one that it had always been: Bonneville Ranch. It was the home she'd been born to, the home she deserved.

As she burst through the front door of Solomon's house, she forced herself not to look to closely at the beginning efforts to decorate it that she'd engaged in for the past two weeks. She forced herself not to breath in the comforting scent of new fabric and hints of cooking, and especially not the all-too-familiar scent of Solomon. None of this should be hers anymore. She leaned back against the closed front door and wept—for the terrible decisions she'd made, for the way she'd broken her promise to her mother, for everything that could have been. She hadn't really believed she was dying before, but she did now. This whole beautiful life was over.

Once she had cried herself out, she headed upstairs to pack her things. She couldn't stay with Solomon now. He would be furious with her when she learned the truth—just as everyone was always furious with her in the end—so it was better to be prepared. She only packed the things she'd brought with her to the marriage, which wasn't much. The few gowns and pieces of jewelry that Solomon had bought for her in the past few weeks belonged to him. The only thing she couldn't bear to part with were her wedding and engagement rings.

With the packing done, she set about cleaning the house. It wouldn't be right to leave it in any sort of a mess when she left. That would only add more insult to the terrible injury she'd done him. But the more she cleaned, the heavier her limbs and heart got.

When Solomon finally came home that evening, he found her sitting at the kitchen table, listless and pale.

"Honoria!" He'd walked into the kitchen with the slow, somber steps of a man whose business was in trouble, but dashed the last few feet to her like a man who cared. Maybe like a man who loved her.

It broke Honoria's heart.

"Sweetheart, what's wrong?" He sank to a crouch beside her chair, smoothing a hand over her hair and cradling her hot face in his hands. "Are you...are you feeling ill?"

If she hadn't been before, she was now, though not in the way he assumed. Her stomach turned over the thought that all of this concern was for a deathly illness that she didn't have. She struggled to speak, struggled not to fly out of her skin to escape the pain that threatened to consume her.

"I..."

"Never mind." With one, smooth movement, Solomon lifted her out of her chair, turned to sit himself, then cradled her in his arms. He held her close, arms closed protectively around her, kissing her forehead, her nose, her lips.

It was heaven and hell at the same time. Right or wrong, she wanted nothing more than to stay there in his arms, to curl up against him and let him continue to believe she was dying and that his horrible losses were all for a good cause after all. Weak though it made her, she buried her head against his shoulder and hugged him.

After a long, tragic silence, Solomon murmured, "We both knew there would be bad days eventually."

Her heart ached in her chest. There would be plenty more bad days for her after she did the right thing and left him, but at least his life would get better. His business would go back to normal, his finances would thrive, and the bitter, bigoted men of the world would only glare at him instead of attacking him outright. He'd been so willing to sacrifice himself to help her, now it was her turn to sacrifice for him.

"Why don't we go over to the hotel for supper tonight," Solomon suggested after more silence.

Honoria shook her head against his neck. "No, I want to stay here." The words were more true than he would ever know.

"All right." He smiled and kissed her forehead. "Are you sure you're up to fixing supper, though?"

Dredging up every last bit of courage she had, she lifted her head and nodded with a weak smile. "Let's cook something together."

His grin widened and he laughed. "Sounds like the perfect activity to bring a little humor into an otherwise gloomy day."

She did her best to laugh with him, but her heart was breaking into pieces. She would always remember that about him, his optimistic attitude and willingness to see the good side of things. Although she was honor-bound to set him free and lift the pressure of prejudice from his shoulders, she would give herself this one last evening of happiness. One last evening to carry in her heart during all those times ahead when things would be wretched.

"I can try making biscuits again." She worked to get the pitifulness out of her voice. "I bet I can get them to come out better than last time."

"There wasn't anything wrong with them last time," Solomon laughed. "Well, not much."

They stood and swayed into motion. Honoria headed to the pantry to fetch flour, lard, and salt for the biscuits while Solomon stepped outside to the root cellar to bring up the chicken they'd bought the day before. For just a while, it was easy to pretend that nothing was wrong, that the world hadn't just come crashing down, and that Solomon's feelings toward her wouldn't change completely as soon as he found out what she'd done.

"What do you think?" he asked after settling the chicken in the roasting pan. "Just salt and pepper and a little olive oil, or should we try out that spice mix you found in the cookbook the other day?" His smile was so genuine, so relaxed.

"Whatever you want," she replied, trying not to break down into tears as she did. If this evening was meant to be the memory she took with her to warm the rest of her dark days, then it should be the kernel of goodness Solomon could hark back to in the moments that he wasn't cursing her name for ruining him.

Unaware of her thoughts, he nodded. "Spices it is."

They went on with their cooking, Solomon chatting animatedly about everything going on in town except the trouble at his bank. He mentioned a story Luke Chance had told him about his and Eden's son. He recounted the positive developments in keeping the peace that Sheriff Knighton had shared with him. He even had a cute story about some trouble Athos Strong's children had gotten into while pretending they were musketeers. Honoria smiled and laughed along, but inside she wilted.

When they finally sat down to eat, Solomon reached for her hands across the table. He lowered his head and closed his eyes before saying, "Lord, we thank you for the boundless gifts you've given us. We thank you for the beautiful time we have together, no matter how short it might be."

After that, Honoria could barely choke down her food. The only thing that consoled her was knowing that after she left he would see that she was truly sorry and had never meant any harm. If she was brave, she would tell him right away, as they cleaned up their simple feast, but that one last, selfish part of her craved a final memory to take away with her.

"If you'd like, we can keep reading *Around the World in Eighty Days*," Solomon suggested once the last dish was dried and put away. He slipped an arm around Honoria's waist and drew her close. "I, for one, am desperate to find out if Phineas Fogg is able to rescue that Indian princess," he added with a fond grin, kissing her lightly.

How was she ever going to summon the courage to do the honorable thing? And how would she bear Solomon's wrath once he learned the truth?

"What if the Indian princess was lying about having to throw herself on the raja's funeral pyre?" she asked, her voice choked.

Solomon furrowed his brow, giving her a strange look. "But she wasn't. It's the custom in India for the wife of a royal man to die with him."

"Is it?" She lowered her head, watching as her fingers pressed into the fabric of his shirt over the broad muscles of his chest.

"I think so." He didn't sound so certain. "I'll admit, I don't know much about the Hindu religion." He brushed his fingers under her chin and lifted it so that she faced him. "What is that question all about? Are you worried I'll fling myself into your grave when…" He swallowed.

Honoria squeezed her eyes shut. She could easily argue that he'd already done something destructive for her sake. How would he feel once he'd jumped into her grave only to discover the coffin was empty?

"Maybe we should start another book," he said, a touch of humor back in his voice. "Something by Mark Twain."

Honoria shook her head, gazing up at him with a burst of passion. "I don't want to sit and read." She pressed herself into him, running her hands down his sides to his hips.

Heat flared behind his eyes and he leaned down to kiss her, but stopped when his lips were inches from hers.

"Are you certain you're feeling up to this?" The tone of his voice—rough and tantalizing—hinted that he hoped she was.

"Yes," she breathed. "Absolutely." She lifted onto her toes to close the remaining distance between them. Her mouth met his hungrily and she sighed audibly. This was the last time she would ever feel the undiluted bliss of being with her husband.

Solomon kissed her back, cautiously at first, but with increasing ardor as the passion between them built. He circled his hands around to stroke her sides, then up to cup her breasts. Even through the layers of fabric and boning of her corset, his touch was magical. Her body responded powerfully, even more so knowing that there was no physical reason whatsoever for her to hold back.

"Take me to bed, Solomon," she entreated him. "And don't hold back."

"How could I?" he whispered in return, then lifted her into his arms. It wasn't the sweet, comforting hold of a man sweeping his frail wife into his arms. He lifted her from her backside, encouraging her to wrap her legs around his waist as he pushed himself forward.

He tried to kiss her as they crossed the kitchen and the hall, but laughed as they both realized walking and kissing at the same time was too awkward. Instead, he rushed around the corner and up the stairs. That laughter continued as they reached the bedroom and he attempted to kiss her again while holding her still. He was strong, and she was light, but with him supporting her, there was only so much their hands could do. And she wanted his hands on her as much as his lips.

"Hold onto that fire," he chuckled as he eased her down to her feet. "Don't let it go, do you hear me?"

Honoria nodded, blinking to fight back tears. He couldn't know what he was saying, couldn't feel how deeply she would need to hold onto not only the fire, but this moment. Forever.

"Getting undressed is always the tedious part." He pretended to sigh as he set to work removing his clothes.

She fumbled with the fastenings of her skirt and bodice, silently agreeing with him. She wanted to watch him undress one last time, watch every inch of his smooth, dark skin as it was revealed to her. But more than that, she wanted to be rid of her own clothes, to be naked and free, available for him to caress and kiss and mold. She didn't even take the time to fold her clothes and set them aside the way he was. It was all she could do to shed them and kick them aside, then tumble into his bed and onto her back to wait for him.

"My, my, you're eager tonight," he growled with tender appreciation as he removed his trousers. His lighthearted humor was swiftly melting into molten passion.

"I want you," she whispered. Shameless as she knew she was, she let her knees drop to the side and lifted her arms to pull the pins out of her hair, giving him the fullest view of her that she could.

All remaining teasing vanished, and powerful desire filled his expression. She was rewarded with the sight of his manhood standing thick and tall and ready as he stepped out of his trousers and kicked them aside. Even after two weeks, he still inspired a quivering need in her that bordered on fear. It wasn't fear of him, though. Not in the least. It was the fear of how wanton she found herself to be, how desperately she wanted to feel every hot inch of him slide home within her.

"Come to me," she murmured, shaking her hair free. It fell in tangled waves around her as she held her arms out to him.

Solomon groaned as he surged toward the bed, crawling over top of her. She sighed in victory as his large, heavy body covered hers, skin embracing skin and setting her alight. He fit so well against her. Her arms and legs caressed his contours. His mouth was ravenous as it met hers, parting her lips with just enough force to be daring. His tongue danced against hers in teasing miniature of what she wanted a much greater part of him to do.

*I love you*, she cried out in her heart, feeling every word as though it were a grain of her soul. *I love you, Solomon, and I will always love you, no matter what you come to think of me*. She wanted to say those words out loud, scream them if she had to, but releasing that kind of truth would only make tomorrow worse.

Instead she shouted without words as his hand raked up her side and found her breast. She was so ready for that touch that the pleasure of it felt magnified a thousand-fold. He curled his fingers up to rake her nipple, then pinched lightly. She felt the snap of sensation all the way through her, down to the aching muscles of her core.

"Honoria," Solomon growled, heavy with emotion. He nibbled a trail of kisses down her neck, over her collarbone, and lower across her chest. The friction of his body shifting lower so that his mouth came level with her breasts was almost as good as the heat of his breath against her sensitive skin.

He pressed her breast up to meet his lips and teeth, and Honoria gasped with the pleasure of it. It didn't matter that she'd felt the sensation from him before. This would be the last time he ever suckled her, the last time she dug her nails into his back to show her delight. He responded so well to her needs without her having to say a word, so much so that she felt as though she was on the brink of exploding without him even coming near the part of her that really burned for him.

And then, when he shifted to her other breast and closed his mouth over her, sucking hard, she did burst. It was so sudden that she moaned in ecstasy, arching against him. She was wild to mate with him, feel him pumping hard inside of her right then and there, but as much as she writhed to bring some part of her that was throbbing into contact with him, he continued his attention to her breasts without even noticing her orgasm.

The tremors began to subside as he moved away from her breasts and down across her stomach, but whatever fear she had that her body was done was quickly squashed. He rained kisses across the flat of her stomach and abdomen, shifting again to expose her primed and wet core, and another wave of needy aching rose up behind her first release.

"I love you like this," Solomon rumbled, his eyes raking her. "I shouldn't say it because it's not proper, but seeing you spread out and glistening with passion like this, in my bed, does things to me that you'll never know."

As if to prove his point, he lifted himself higher to get a better view and traced his hands from her sides, down over her hips, and across her thighs as if sculpting her. She was beyond finding words to tell him how much she loved his touch and his eyes on her, but sighed and mewled and lifted her arms above her head in sweet surrender as he did. She watched the play of his fingers as they inched their way possessively up her thighs, teasing but not quite touching the folds that were hungry for him. The feeling of being laid out for his pleasure was almost beyond what she could bear.

Her gaze drifted past his hands, up his arms, and down his chest to spy his staff, erect against his abdomen as he knelt between her legs. She knew what that powerful part of him felt like inside of her, and she bit her lip in anticipation. There was something so primal, so delicious about seeing him fully engorged and ready to take her that her legs trembled. She wanted to run her hands over him, take him into her mouth and learn everything she could about how he felt and tasted. So what if it made her brazen.

Her thoughts scattered as he teased his fingers up into her folds at last. She let out a gasping sigh as he slipped one and then two fingers inside of her. The dizzying rhythm of his touch was matched only by the look of intense desire in his eyes as he watched his handiwork. She arched her hips into him, spread her legs wider so he could see. For the second time, her body flared and raced toward completion. Her breathing came harder, and she cried out more wildly the closer she came.

At last, he withdrew his fingers and teased them upward, spreading her folds as he grazed and then rubbed the focal point of her pleasure. It was too, too perfect. She broke apart again, muscles contracting under his impassioned gaze. There was something so intimate about him watching her lose herself in pleasure of his making that the tremors kept coming and coming. He groaned in triumph at the sight, then dipped forward to kiss and lick the very nub that had begun the orgasm.

His kiss was just a prelude, though. With almost predatory desire, he inched his way back up her body, then drove himself home inside of her. Honoria cried out with pleasure and clasped her arms and legs around him. He wasn't gentle—though he was far from hurting her—and with each thrust his breathing became more ragged, the sounds he made more primal. He filled her so completely, moving in her so hard and fast that she lost track of where she ended and he began. She felt both as if she was completely at his mercy and as if he were a wild beast that only she could control as he mated with her.

She could feel his tension rising and his body getting ready to explode inside of her and reached down to dig her fingernails into his backside. She loved every tight contour of that part of him and knew that her nails would throw him over the edge. Sure enough, he cried out as she gripped him, and his whole body went tense. She encouraged him to continue to thrust as his seed flowed into her, though he quickly lost momentum and energy.

Finally, he sighed and collapsed on top of her, too stunned to pull out of her right away. Not only did she not mind, she loved that moment, just after he finished, when he was too weak and too spent to move. She loved that feeling that he'd given so much of himself to her that for a moment or two he had nothing left to push away from her. His weight, the force of his breathing, the heat of his body…all were things she would treasure as much as the way he made her feel. She held onto them especially hard, embracing him for all she was worth as he drifted in the afterglow. This was the way she wanted to remember him.

# Chapter Thirteen

For the first time in more than a week, Solomon woke up with a deep confidence and a sense that the worst was over. The WSGA had made their crooked determination about his business and he'd paid their fine, even though it was extortion. His assets had been obliterated. There was nowhere else to turn for cash. But at least the bank had made it through the storm. He ran through the list of his remaining customers as he dressed for the day, certain that no one left would demand to withdraw all of their money.

Now he could focus on his real purpose—at least his purpose for as long as it lasted. It was time to do his utmost to make Honoria happy and comfortable to the end.

A bittersweet grin touched his lips as he straightened his tie and headed out of their bedroom and downstairs to the tempting smell of bacon. Breakfast wasn't the only tempting thing in the house. No matter how many times he told himself that he should take it easy in bed with his delicate wife, she turned things around on him. Honoria was insatiable, in spite of her illness. And while something tickled at the back of his mind, telling him that wasn't quite right for a consumptive, he was far too pleased with the way things happened so naturally between the two of them. Besides, Honoria was the instigator of their passion as often as not. He would wait and watch and be ready for the day that she decided enough was enough.

"Good morning, sweetheart." He greeted her with a kiss as he entered the kitchen. Honoria was already setting plates heaped with bacon and eggs and buttered toast on the table. She'd become an amazing cook in just two weeks, but then, he figured Honoria was clever enough to become an expert at anything she set her mind to.

"Coffee will be done in just a second," she murmured and turned away from him.

Solomon's joy flattened. He grabbed his chair but studied Honoria before sitting. Was she looking a little pale today? She was certainly avoiding his eyes. Maybe he had been too exuberant last night after all. She *was* ill, after all. He cursed himself for not being more careful.

"I was thinking that we could go for a long drive and a relaxing picnic closer to the mountains on Saturday," he said, sitting and taking up his fork. "With all the fuss here in town, it would be nice to go somewhere where it could just be the two of us."

She didn't answer. She kept her face turned so that he couldn't see, but it was obvious that her shoulders were rock hard. If he wasn't mistaken, she lowered her head and gulped as if…as if holding back tears. Concern that bordered on panic gripped him.

"Honoria, are you *sure* you're feeling all right?" he asked, hoping his tone was tender and not overly anxious. "Maybe you should go talk to Dr. Meyers."

"I'm fine." She sucked in a breath and straightened

all at once, twisting to face him. The smile she wore looked brittle enough to snap, and her eyes were glassy. "Let me get your coffee."

Deep foreboding settled in Solomon's gut, making even the delicious breakfast Honoria had prepared taste like ash. Something was wrong, more wrong than he knew what to do with. Honoria brought his coffee and some for herself and sat across from him, but she did little more than push her food around her plate with her fork. Her cheeks were alternately pale and flushed as the thoughts he could see but not name flashed across her features. He had to be able to do something about this, anything.

"Do you want me to come over to Wendy's at lunchtime to take you for a walk?" he asked lamely, bristling with the need to do something.

Honoria shook her head, not meeting his eyes. "No, that's all right, I'll be fine." She choked on the word "fine" and pressed her hand to her mouth.

It was her illness. It had to be. Somehow it had gotten worse and she hadn't been able to tell him about it. She was scared, obviously. Anyone would be. Again, he cursed himself for being so energetic last night.

When he finished his breakfast, he reached across the table to take her hand. He had to pry her fingers out of a tight fist to hold it. "I would keep the bank closed or let Horace run it himself today if I could," he said, twining his fingers with hers. "I would let it all go to spend my day in your arms, if not for those blasted WSGA men."

Honoria squeezed her eyes shut and nodded, though she turned her face away from him.

His heart ached and twisted in his chest. "Honoria, are you certain there's nothing you need to tell me? Are you sure you're all right?"

She took a long time to reply…a long time in which

she held herself so tightly that she wasn't breathing. At last she gasped for breath and looked at him. "Please go to work." Her plea was wispy and hoarse. "I know how important your bank is to you. You need to make sure that it's safe."

He wanted to argue with her, to tell her that, first and foremost, he needed to make sure *she* was safe. But he could see the determination in her eyes, sitting just beyond whatever else was bothering her. If he tried to argue, she would dig her heels in. Maybe she needed a little bit of time to think things through or to rest.

Reluctantly, he let her hand go and rose. "Promise me you'll take it easy today, sweetheart." He stepped around the table to kiss her forehead. It was hot. Did she have a fever? "Wendy can spare you for one day. Why don't you stay home and nap?"

She didn't answer, but he thought that her slight nod might have been agreement. He debated staying home to help her and damning the consequences, but she was right about his bank needing him.

"Take care of yourself." He kissed her one last time, then retrieved his jacket from the back of his chair and put it on.

All the way to the bank, he replayed breakfast, looking for hints about Honoria's health that he hadn't seen before. She hadn't been that shy with him since before their wedding. Had he said something wrong, either that morning or the night before? He second-guessed everything he'd done, every word that he'd spoken to her in the last day and more. Something wasn't right, as if there was a detail out of place. She was keeping something from him.

"Ah, Solomon, thank heavens you're here." Horace snapped up from the work he was doing behind the bank's counter as soon as he walked through the door. "I've been reviewing the remaining accounts, and I think I have some good news."

Solomon's worries about Honoria were pushed to the side as he dove into work for the day. Horace had opened a whole new ledger and begun to record the cash on hand versus the remaining accounts. Though things were bad — no two ways about that — there was hope on the horizon. Not only were the vast majority of the accounts remaining held by customers who Solomon was certain would never turn on him, the morning newspaper — or rather yesterday's newspaper from Denver, brought in on the late train the night before — had good news about the handful of stocks Solomon hadn't sold.

He was just beginning to think that the storm was past and he would be able to recover when the door flew open. Solomon's heart sank as the WSGA men sauntered into the lobby.

"Good morning, gentlemen." He stood, keeping his back straight and clasping his hands behind him. "Is there anything I can do for you?"

"Nope," Eastman answered with a smirk.

"We're just here to monitor," Lamb added, his expression as suspiciously giddy as Eastman's.

"I can assure you that the bank's business practices will continue today as they have every day, as you've already observed them," Solomon answered, willing himself to keep calm. Clearly the men were up to something.

"We'll be the judge of that," O'Brien added with a sniff.

They stood there. Just stood there, staring at him. Solomon stared right back, working to figure out what kind of intimidation technique this was. They didn't appear to be armed. Even if they were, Trey Knighton and Travis Montrose were "on duty" outside of the bank that day. There were no customers in the bank either, though it had been open for more than an hour. The money was all counted and accounted for. Everything seemed fine.

Which didn't explain why the hair on the back of his neck was standing up.

He had to wait another half hour, until it was past eleven o'clock, to discover why the men were there. At first, it was just one man, Matthew Bolton, the saddle-maker.

"Morning, Matthew." Solomon greeted him with a smile as he entered, head lowered. "Come to make your weekly deposit?"

"Uh, no," Matthew mumbled. He shuffled up to the counter, shoulders stooped. "I, uh, I gotta withdraw all my money from your bank."

Alarm bells sounded in Solomon's head. Matthew was one of the Haskell tradesmen he never would have imagined turning on him. In fact, he didn't believe Matthew had turned of his own free will. His body language told another story.

"Horace has the appropriate forms for you to sign," Solomon said, nodding to Horace.

Matthew muttered his thanks, then filled out the form as Horace counted out enough cash to cover the withdrawal, face drawn. Solomon crossed his arms and narrowed his eyes at the WSGA men. They didn't seem at all surprised by the turn of events.

If Matthew had been the only one to turn on him, Solomon would have considered it a minor disappointment, but a few minutes later, two more of Haskell's tradesmen—John Bimeney, the cooper and Paul Lindy, the carpenter who split his time between several towns in the county—dragged themselves in to withdraw everything. These were men Solomon would never have guessed would betray him, men he considered his friends. It was small relief that he was able to pay out what needed to be paid out.

"I don't like this at all," Horace muttered once the two men had gone. "It ain't right."

"No, it isn't," Solomon replied. He sent another look to the WSGA men. Their silent waiting took on a more sinister feel. They were waiting for the money to run out, waiting like they knew it would happen soon. Once it did, they would arrest him. He wasn't fool enough to think that he'd be able to get out of that.

The door slammed open in the middle of his grim thoughts, and Sam Standish marched in. "It's an outrage!" he hollered.

Of all things, Sam's indignation came as a relief to Solomon. He was certain beyond any shadow of doubt that Sam would never, ever betray him. But if he knew what was going on—

"Bonneville's sending his thugs around to all the local businesses," Sam told him, marching up and gripping the edge of the counter. "He's threatening to take his business elsewhere and to tell his friends and neighbors to do the same if they continue to use your bank."

"He can't do that," Horace gasped.

The WSGA men grinned from ear to ear, as if none of this was even remotely a surprise.

"That's a lot of business for the tradesmen of this town to lose." Solomon sighed, rubbing a hand across his face. It was all beginning to make sense. If Rex Bonneville couldn't destroy him one way, he would find another. "Men like Matthew and John and Paul can't survive if they're blacklisted by Bonneville."

"It ain't right," Horace wailed.

"Oh, look," Eastman blurted, craning his neck to look out the window at the front of the bank. "There's a whole bunch of them coming."

Solomon swallowed, balling his hands into fists. This was it. This was the end of his bank, and quite possibly the end of his life.

"Want me to fetch Howard?" Sam offered. "Or Gunn?"

If the end was coming, then Solomon was determined to face it head-on and not run crying for help. "No." He straightened his back as the bank door opened and more than half a dozen men shuffled in. "I've asked them for too much already. It's time I faced this on my own."

"But—"

Sam was cut off when Eastman stepped forward. "You gents here to withdraw your money?" He looked as though he was having the best day of his life.

"Yes," one of the tradesmen answered.

"Mmm hmm," another one mumbled, looking as though he might be sick.

Solomon knew each and every one of these men. They were entrepreneurs, friends, men who had come West to build their fortunes, the same as he had. They worked hard, played for the Haskell baseball teams, went to church with him. Not a single one of them could survive if Bonneville and his cronies stopped doing business with them.

"Gentlemen," Solomon addressed them grimly. "I understand. And I'll do my best by you."

He was met by guilty silence and a few grunts of grudging appreciation. None of the men looked at him, and none of them looked at the smiling, smug, supercilious WSGA men.

"Horace, give these men withdrawal forms," Solomon ordered.

"But, Solomon…"

Solomon sighed and thumped his faithful employee on the back, then answered in a sad voice, "Just do it."

Horace lowered his head, knowing full well what it meant as he reached for the forms with shaking hands. "It ain't right," he muttered as he distributed the forms to the men who lined the counter.

No, it wasn't right, but it was the way of the world. At least for now.

In the middle of the gloom of defeat, the bank door banged open once again. Solomon snapped his head up to see what new misery had come for him. The other men gasped, and the WSGA men gaped as Pearl, Domenica, Della, and all of the other girls from Bonnie's place pushed their way into the lobby. The small space wasn't designed for so many people, and the girls seemed to take up twice as much room as the others. They were all dressed colorfully, their bodices so low-cut it was a wonder none of them started to spill out, their skirts hiked and tied to show off a good amount of leg. The crushing scent of flowers and powder and sweetness filled the room with them. They dealt with the cramped conditions by pressing up against the men—tradesmen and WSGA men alike—simpering and batting their eyelashes.

"Ladies," Solomon addressed them. "I'm sorry, but you'll have to wait your turn to withdraw your money."

The girls all giggled and cooed, the ones who were pressed against the men fondling their collars…or something lower, judging by the way Grover Holmes yelped then laughed.

"Oh, silly." Pearl stepped up to the counter, reaching into her bodice and taking out a surprisingly large wad of cash from between her ample breasts. "We're not here to take money out, we're here to *put it in*. Right boys?"

The girls laughed and whooped, and the men guffawed along with them, eyes zooming to all the places they probably shouldn't have in public. Della even tilted her chest forward and asked one of the tradesmen, "You wanna reach in there and get my cash for me, honey?"

In an instant, the mood in the bank had utterly changed. The men who had come to withdraw their money were distracted beyond thought. Bonnie's girls pushed past them to the counter, managing to flutter and flirt while making several impressively large piles of bills on the table.

"Bonnie's always telling us we should deposit our earnings in the bank," Pearl told Solomon, an exceptionally shrewd look in her bright blue eyes. "I figure it's about time we opened those accounts."

"But don't you already have an account?" Horace asked, slack-jawed and more interested in what was almost popping out of Pearl's bodice than her cash.

"These are *special* accounts," Pearl answered. Her sharp gaze shifted to Solomon. "Bonnie says so."

Bonnie. Everything clicked in Solomon's mind. This money came from Bonnie. Some of it might have belonged to the girls, but whores, no matter how well-paid and taken care of, wouldn't have the kind of money the girls were plopping on the table. Bonnie did well on her own, but everyone in town knew exactly where Bonnie got the bulk of her money from—Rex Bonneville.

A wide grin slowly grew on Solomon's face and in his chest. Going to Howard and Gunn for help was obvious. Asking Bonnie to help him beard the lion in his den was a stroke of genius that he never would have thought of.

"Horace, give these ladies forms to open new

accounts," Solomon boomed as loud as Howard on a good day. "Then help me count this cash."

"But you can't do that," Eastman protested. He tried to reach around Domenica to drag himself to the counter, but Domenica stood firmly in his way, hands roving his body. When Eastman let out a blood-curdling, high-pitched shriek, Solomon was pretty sure she'd grabbed hold of him where it counted and would keep him in his place more effectively than any revolver.

The door opened again, and more sad-faced, Haskell tradesmen wandered in. They blinked in surprise at the scene that was unfolding.

"And another thing," Pearl went on as if in the middle of giving an Independence Day speech. She went so far as to hop up onto the counter, then to stand, lifting her skirts and shaking them. "Me and all the girls over at Bonnie's have decided that from here on out, we're only gonna do business with men who have accounts with this here bank." The other girls whooped and hollered. "Because it's only a good time if we're all good and responsible, right girls?"

"Right!" they responded in unison, shimmying and hugging the men closest to them.

Solomon had a hard time not laughing out loud at the shift in events.

"You…you mean you won't entertain us *at all* if we don't have our money in this bank?" one of the tradesmen stammered.

"Not…not even a little slap and tickle?" another squeaked.

"Nope." Pearl smiled proudly, dancing a few steps on the counter. "And you boys all know how far it is to the next cathouse."

The girls laughed and made noises like it was a

journey around the world. The tradesmen gawped and shook their heads, looking to each other for help and answers and finding none. The WSGA men could only stand back and glower...though Eastman could barely even do that with Domenica still in full possession of his...faculties.

"That's it." Grover reached for the withdrawal form he'd started to fill out and ripped it to pieces. "Rex can strong-arm me all he wants, but some things are sacred. I'll just have to work twice as hard to court new customers."

"That's the spirit, honey." One of the girls rushed to hug him. "Why don't we go across the street to celebrate?"

Within minutes, the whirlwind of Bonnie's girls circled through the bank as each one filled out a form for a new account as best they could, then grabbed a man and headed off to help them put their money to better use. Solomon went to work by Horace's side, helping the girls fill out the forms and counting the cash. Bonnie had outdone herself. Whether all of the money came from Bonneville directly or not, there was more than enough to fill the cash drawer. Word must have spread about the girls' ultimatum too, because within an hour, most of the men who had withdrawn their money that morning returned to put it back.

Eastman and the other WSGA cronies got angrier and angrier as the morning wore into afternoon, but there was nothing they could do. Finally, they gave up and left. Solomon prayed it would be the last he saw of them, but doubted it. At least he could be sure of one thing—his bank was safe.

"I've got to tell Honoria about this," he said as he and Horace finished counting the drawer in the middle of the afternoon. "She won't believe it."

"I'm not sure I believe it myself," Horace laughed. Solomon thumped him on the back. "You go tell the story to that pretty wife of yours. I'll keep the bank open until closing. Something tells me it won't be as busy for the rest of the day."

"I hope not!" Solomon shook his hand, then grabbed his hat and headed out to the street, grinning like a Cheshire cat.

If Honoria had taken his advice, she'd be at home resting. He headed there first, but was, admittedly, unsurprised when he didn't find her napping on the sofa or in their bed, as he would have liked. His wife was industrious and determined, if nothing else. He assumed she had gone to work after all and headed out again to Wendy's shop.

"Honoria?" he called as he walked through the shop's front door, bell jingling.

"Hello?" Wendy answered his call. A moment later, she stepped out from the back room, her and Travis's sweet baby boy in her arms. "Solomon!"

"Good afternoon, Mrs. Montrose." Solomon removed his hat and nodded. He couldn't wipe the grin from his face. "I wonder if I might have a word with my beautiful wife?"

Wendy blinked at him. "She didn't come into work today."

As Wendy's expression pinched to worry, so did Solomon's. "She didn't?"

"No, sir." Wendy shook her head. "I haven't seen her since yesterday morning."

Solomon frowned. "She's not at home. I was certain she would have come to work."

Wendy shrugged. "She didn't."

The panic from that morning that he had forgotten

about in the midst of his wild day returned full-force. He tried to mask it with a neighborly smile. "I suppose I'll have to look for her somewhere else."

"Let me know if you need any help," Wendy said.

Solomon turned to go, fixing his hat back on his head as he stepped outside. Where could Honoria have gone?

The answer hit him with a bitter twist of regret. To Dr. Meyers, of course. She wasn't feeling well. She hadn't been willing to worry him with the details, but he was sure of it. Of course she would have gone to see the doctor.

He launched into motion, hurrying down Main Street and around the corner to practically run up Prairie Avenue. Dr. Meyers's house and office was halfway up the street, so by the time he reached it, he was out of breath. That didn't stop him from taking the steps two at a time and bursting into the office.

"Oh!" Abigail exclaimed as Solomon entered.

"Is my wife here?" Solomon asked without greeting.

"Your wife? Oh!"

She didn't have time to get any farther before Dean Meyers stepped out of his office. "Solomon," he said with a wide smile, rushing forward to shake Solomon's hand. "I hear congratulations are in order."

"Yes, sir," he answered, too distracted to really hear them. "Is my wife here? She seemed to be feeling poorly this morning."

"Poorly?" Dean frowned, more confused than sympathetic. "That's strange."

Solomon narrowed his eyes, as confused as Dean. "Not so strange, considering her condition."

Dean's eyes went wide. "You mean, she didn't tell you?"

Panic made the corners of Solomon's vision go black. "Didn't tell me what?"

Completely inexplicably, Dean beamed as though Solomon had won a prize at the county fair. "Didn't tell you that she's not sick."

"What?" Solomon's heart stopped completely. His whole body began to vibrate on a minute level.

"She's perfectly healthy. Dr. Abernathy confused her file with that of another woman who has consumption."

"*What*?" The breath squeezed out of his lungs. He hardly dared to hope that what Dean was telling him was true.

"Yes, I'm so pleased to tell you that Honoria is the picture of health. Her coughing was merely the result of stress, probably from the situation at home. That is, at her father's home. She looked quite well when she was here yesterday."

The words were having a hard time to sink in to Solomon's soul. Probably because he couldn't believe that he would ever be so lucky. Honoria wasn't dying. She was his, his very own, and she wasn't going to leave him. They had an entire life ahead of them, a long, happy, fruitful life.

He loved her. The second realization hit him harder than the first. He had always been fond of her. He cared for her. She filled him with fire when they were in bed. He hadn't dared to let himself give his heart over and to actually love her. But he did. More than anything he had ever loved or ever would love. And he could love her as much as he wanted for years to come.

Where was she?

"I'm sorry, Dean. I have to go find my wife." He barely managed to push the words out before turning and running from the office.

Where could she have gone? If she wasn't dying and if she *knew* she wasn't dying, where would she be? And why hadn't she told him last night?

He skidded to a stop at the bottom of Prairie Avenue as the realization hit him. She hadn't told him last night, and she'd known the truth. Why? Why wouldn't she tell him something so amazingly, blissfully wonderful?

Reason took over from elation and he pushed himself into motion again, heading home. If there was an answer, logic told him that it would be at home, in the private space they shared. Honoria was too good, too noble to run off without telling him something or leaving him some clue. He had to have missed something when he'd looked for her at the house earlier.

Sure enough, as he raced through the house looking for signs, he found a note folded on the kitchen counter. He hadn't thought to look in the kitchen when he assumed she'd be napping. He snatched the note up and read it.

"*Dearest Solomon. Words cannot express how deeply I regret putting you through the nightmare of everything that has happened to you in these last few weeks. You are a good, noble, wonderful man, and my heart will belong to you always. If I had known that my simple, selfish request would have caused such devastation in your life, I would never have asked. Please believe me when I say that I never meant to hurt you. I never meant for your business to be ruined or for you to endure everything that has happened. If I could turn back time and prevent it, I would.*

"*For you see, I've only just found out that I am not dying after all. There was a mistake with files, and I was given someone else's diagnosis. I regret terribly that I forced you to marry me under false pretenses, and now that it has come out that I am not dying, that the whole reason for me asking you to marry me, care for me, and fill my last days with happiness has proven to be a lie, I am beyond devastated. Please believe me that*

*I had no intention to deceive you. I may not have a fatal disease, but it is killing me inside to know that I have been the sole cause of so much misery to you.*

"I can only imagine how much you hate me right now, but I swear to you that I did not know that my death was a lie. You will probably resent me to the end of your days for everything that has happened. I cannot bear to see it, to know that you think badly of me. So I've gone home to my father's house. It's where I belong, and it's what I deserve. I can only hope that you'll find it in your heart to forgive me someday. Yours, Honoria."

"Oh my darling." Solomon let out a heavy breath and sank into the kitchen chair. His heart ached as though it had burst in his chest. How could she think that he would ever hate her? It was an honest mistake, someone else's honest mistake at that. Why would she assume that this was her fault?

Because of Bonneville. The answer came to him with swift fury. Bonneville and his spoiled daughters had taught Honoria that she was inconsequential at best and the cause of everything bad at worst. He should have seen that her past was more of a burden to her than she'd let on. Two weeks of freedom barely began to make up for a lifetime of emotional slavery. He knew that as well as anyone. How long had it taken him to grow past the mindset of belonging to someone else?

He wouldn't stand for it. Tossing the letter on the table, he shot out of his seat and bolted down the hall to the back door and the stable where his horse was kept. There were more important things to save than banks and careers. The time had come for him to save his wife.

# *Chapter Fourteen*

Walking all the way from Haskell to her father's ranch while carrying a stuffed carpetbag was a crucial part of Honoria's self-imposed penance for the trouble she'd caused. She was certain that she deserved every blister that would well up on her feet, every sore muscle in her arms and back, and every bit of dust that ruined the bottom of her skirt. She didn't expect to feel a strange sense of pride in herself and strength—not to mention wonder—that she was able to make the entire miles-long trek without stopping to rest. She had grown in so many ways since leaving to marry Solomon.

Before she knew it, she was imagining the way he would smile at her and tell her how brave she was for making the journey all by herself. She couldn't shake the vision of his surprisingly straight teeth and dark, dancing eyes. That only led to cozy memories of the way his body enveloped hers when she curled against him, the way they fit so well together in the throes of passion.

By the time she crossed through the gate at the edge of her father's property and started down the drive toward the house, the voice at the back of her head was whispering that she'd made a terrible mistake to leave without at least discussing things with Solomon face-to-face. Returning home was just another bad idea in a string of bad ideas.

"Oh my gosh, is that *Honoria*?" Bebe was the first one to see her. All three sisters sat on the front porch, fanning themselves in the afternoon heat and sipping some sort of cool beverages. "It *is* Honoria!"

Bebe jumped away from Vivian and Melinda. It was only then that Honoria noticed Bebe wasn't lounging and fanning herself like the other two. She was sewing something. Not only that, instead of wearing one of her usual flouncy dresses, she'd put on one of Honoria's shabby old work dresses.

"Honoria?" Melinda shot to her feet, squinting as she searched to see what Bebe saw.

Vivian leapt up a moment later, and within seconds, the three sisters were racing down off of the porch to meet her.

"Oh, Honoria! I'm *so* happy to see you. You can't even imagine." Bebe slammed into her with a hug that caused Honoria to drop her carpetbag. For a second, Honoria couldn't tell if her younger sister was laughing or weeping.

"Get off of her!" Vivian yelled, charging toward them with a straight back. "Honestly, Bebe. What sort of an idiot are you? Only a nitwit puts on displays like that."

"Stupid cow." Melinda sniffed. She crossed her arms as she came close to Honoria.

Bebe gasped and leapt back, straightening her skirt with jerky movements. "Sorry, Vivian. I'm so sorry, Melinda. I didn't mean to be a stupid cow. But it's

Honoria." She gulped a few times, almost trembling with tension and misery.

"So? Vivian crossed her arms now too. She tilted her chin up. "What do you want?"

Internally, Honoria second-guessed everything she had been so certain about for the last eighteen hours. In the span of two weeks, Vivian looked older and twice as peevish. Melinda, on the other hand, somehow seemed younger, or perhaps immature was a better word. And Bebe… Well, looking at the strain in Bebe's face made it easy for Honoria to see how she could have developed an anxious cough.

Still, Honoria picked up her carpetbag, squared her shoulders, and said, "I've come home."

The three sisters stared at her, mouths open, Vivian and Melinda wearing calculating frowns.

"Did…did Mr. Templesmith throw you out?" Bebe ventured uncertainly.

"No," Honoria answered with as little emotion as she could. "I left of my own free will."

"Why?" Bebe asked, or rather, implored.

"It's not important." Honoria lowered her head, losing some of her strength under the weight of the destruction she'd caused.

"Ha!" Vivian barked. Her peevish look morphed into a sour smile. "I *knew* Papa would win that fight."

"Papa always wins," Melinda added, equally as smug.

Vivian's smile faded away, leaving her expression just plain bitter. "Don't I know it," she grumbled.

Bebe sent Vivian a wary, sidelong look. Melinda looked as though she'd eaten something spoiled. She and Vivian recovered fast enough for Melinda to say, "Well, I'm glad you're back. I have two new dresses that need to be finished before the Founder's Day ball, and Bebe here is a complete clod with a needle."

Bebe wilted, looking like she might either cry or dissolve into a puddle.

Honoria sighed. "What work still needs to be done?"

Vivian and Melinda took her resignation as their own personal victory.

"The whole thing needs to be taken apart and sewn anew," Melinda said.

"And when you're done with that, this useless piece of nothing can't even get the stains out of my boots, so you'll have to."

"And I'm not going to church again with my best bonnet looking the way it does."

"And no one has tidied my room in ages. Rance is such a pig."

Vivian and Melinda suddenly clammed up at Vivian's final statement as if with some private and dire knowledge. Vivian climbed the porch stairs with the air of a woman going to the gallows, while Melinda darted sidelong glances of horror, mingled with relief that it wasn't her, Vivian's way. They likely thought they were as discreet as could be, but Honoria was certain the theatrics were just another part of Vivian's unhappy marriage.

Before she could think more about it, the front door opened and their father stepped out onto the porch. "I thought I heard your voice," he said without any particular show of emotion one way or another, narrowing his eyes at Honoria. "What are you doing here?"

Honoria took a deep breath—drawing strength from the fact that she *could* take a deep breath—and said, "I've come home, Papa. This is where I belong." She'd planned to keep her explanation as short and simple as possible, but she hadn't planned on the whole thing sounding like a colossal lie. *You* don't *belong here*, that voice in her head whispered.

Her father took a half step back, crossed his arms, and looked her up and down. "What if I don't want a despoiled whore like you living under my roof?"

Bebe gasped. Even Vivian and Melinda looked shocked. Honoria would have loved nothing more than to be surprised by his reaction, but she wasn't.

"I made a mistake," she said. "I...I acted impulsively." That was the truth no matter how you cut it.

Her father continued to stare at her with a sneer. No one on the porch moved. If he turned her away, disowned her entirely, she had no idea where she'd go.

At last, Rex hissed out a breath and uncrossed his arms. "If you stay here, you're going to make yourself useful. There's work to be done, and someone needs to do it."

That much was nothing new. "Yes, Papa."

"You're an embarrassment to the name Bonneville," he went on. "I won't have you swanning around town to remind everyone of it. You don't leave the ranch from here on, and you don't talk to anyone who isn't a family member."

"Yes, Papa." It was what she deserved for all the trouble she'd caused, she reminded herself. And reminded herself again. Something deep within her rejected the notion, screaming out that it was wrong even as she worked to keep her expression penitent and her head lowered.

"You are not to be trusted around men either," Rex went on. "If I so much as see you looking at one, I'll move you to the barracks and let the ranch hands teach you what you're good for."

She snapped her head up, eyes blazing with fury and defiance for a moment. The mere thought of being intimate with any man other than Solomon was sacrilege. That her father would suggest pimping her out to his employees was unconscionable. But she was in no position to argue.

"Yes, Papa," she ground out, jaw clenched.

Rex twisted to look back into the house, his expression annoyed. "Where the devil is Rance anyhow?"

Honoria blinked. Rance? What did he have to do with anything.

"Coming, Uncle Rex!" Rance's shout came from deeper in the house. A few seconds later, Rance stumbled through the front doorway, nearly spilling to his face as he did. Strong liquor fumes followed him. "Uh, what're we doin' again?"

Vivian grunted in disgust and marched down the porch to the arrangement of chairs and chaise. She plopped into the chaise with a dramatic sigh. Melinda followed her, murmuring words of comfort.

"We're riding out to inspect the herd," Rex grumbled, his patience clearly hanging on by a thread.

"Oh, yeah, right." Rance hiccupped.

Rex grabbed him by the lapel of his disheveled jacket and dragged him on, off of the porch and away in the direction of the stables.

It took Honoria a second to realize he'd dismissed her without even finishing the point he'd been making about the rules she should live under, as if, now that she was back where he thought she belonged, she was so unimportant to him that he couldn't even be bothered to discipline her. While that sparked torrents of rage in her—something entirely new when it came to her feelings about her father—it was also an odd relief. He could bluster, but in all likelihood, he wouldn't notice her if she was in front of his face.

"I'll just put my things inside," she said, not sure who she was talking to.

She headed into the house, Bebe lunging after her. "You can't," Bebe said.

"Can't what?" Honoria stopped inside the front hall and turned to her.

"Can't have your old room back, for one. Vivian made it into her parlor." She leaned closer, eyes wide. "Actually, she'd been sleeping in there when she can get away from Cousin Rance." She looked like she wanted to say more, like she wanted to gossip about Vivian and Cousin Rance.

Honoria didn't have the heart for it. She set her carpetbag down in a corner of the hall. "I can sleep on a sofa if I have to."

Bebe rushed to grab her arm. "You can sleep in my room with me." The strength of her grip and distraught hope in her eyes made Honoria feel sorry for her as she never had before.

"Thank you." She smiled and gave her sister a hug.

Vivian and Melinda were right about one thing. There were a mountain of things to be done around the house. Honoria set to work, surprised that Bebe actually deigned to help her. A lot had changed in just two weeks, though, and it looked like Bebe was one of those things. They cleaned Vivian and Melinda's rooms together, fetched them lunch and made lemonade for them, then sat and worked on the sewing that Melinda wanted done.

Vivian and Melinda were in their element with two sisters to bully and push around. Part of Honoria expected Bebe to slip back into her old, obnoxious ways and was surprised when she didn't. Honoria had forced herself to return home as punishment for her sins, but the environment she found was worlds away from the one she'd left. If Bebe had been so helpful years ago instead of aspiring to be as horrid as Vivian and Melinda, Honoria's life at her father's house might have been bearable.

Which would have meant she never would have begged Solomon to marry her.

"Honoria? What are you doing here?" It was late in the afternoon when Bonnie stepped regally up onto the porch where Vivian and Melinda were napping and Honoria and Bebe were sewing. Underneath Bonnie's surprise was a light to her expression and a victorious spark to her eye. "Are you all right? Is something wrong?"

Honoria stood as Bonnie rushed across the porch to check on her. She glanced sideways at Bebe. Vivian and Melinda snoozed on, mouths open, a trickle of saliva running down Vivian's chin. There didn't seem to be any harm in letting slip to Bebe what was going on.

"I'm…I'm fine, Bonnie," she admitted, taking Bonnie's hands when they were offered. "Turns out Dr. Abernathy was looking at the wrong file when he told me I was dying."

Bebe gasped. "You're dying?" She looked as though her world had just crashed around her feet after being turned upside down.

"No, I'm not dying," Honoria told her. She turned back to Bonnie. "I'm not dying. There's nothing wrong with me. Dr. Meyers says my cough was caused by stress. I…I married Solomon under false pretenses and ruined his life for nothing."

"Ruined his life?" Bonnie frowned, then shook her head as though the notion were bizarre. "Honey, I think you *made* his life."

Honoria pulled her hands out of Bonnie's and turned

away. "The only reason Papa went after Solomon is because he dared to marry me. Now the bank is ruined. Everything Solomon loves, I destroyed, and for something that turned out to be a lie."

Bonnie stared at her, mouth half-open for so long that Honoria peeked sideways at her to see what was wrong. The look on Bonnie's face could only be described as incredulous. She shook herself, shifted her weight to her other hip, and said, "Honey, Solomon's bank is just fine."

Honoria blinked and turned fully to her once more. "What?"

"It is?" Bebe echoed, brow rising in hope.

"Yes, it is." Bonnie did a terrible job of hiding the way her lips twitched into a smirk before saying, "Thanks to your father."

"What?" Honoria and Bebe exclaimed at the same time. They were loud enough to rouse Vivian and Melinda from their naps.

"What's going on?" Vivian demanded groggily, sitting up and wiping her chin. "What's *she* doing here?"

"Can't you stay in your whorehouse where you belong?" Melinda added with a grumpy, post-nap scowl.

Bonnie ignored them. "The men from the WSGA and Rex tried to pull one last rotten trick on Solomon."

"Papa?" Melinda mumbled, gazing at something past the group consisting of Bonnie, Honoria, and Bebe.

The three of them ignored her, and Bonnie went on. "Rex somehow bribed all of the honest businessmen in town. Told them he'd refuse to do business with them and encourage his buddies not to do business with them either."

"Oh no." Honoria clutched a hand to her chest. "Those were just the sort of people Solomon was counting on to support him."

"Exactly." Bonnie crossed her arms, expression pinched with anger. "It almost worked too. They were flying over to the bank in droves to withdraw their money."

Honoria shrugged and shook her head. "So what happened? You said the bank was fine."

A wide grin spread across Bonnie's face. "Turns out my girls had a bit of a windfall today, and they all wanted to open bank accounts."

"Windfall?" Bebe scratched her head. "What does that mean?"

"It means they came into some money," Honoria told her, hardly believing it. "How?"

Bonnie shrugged. "I gave them all bonuses."

Still confused, Honoria blinked rapidly and asked, "Where did you get the money."

"Where do you think?" Bonnie drawled.

"Papa!" Vivian jumped to their feet behind them.

"More than that," Bonnie went on, still ignoring Vivian and Melinda, "they decided that they wouldn't entertain any man who doesn't have a bank account. That was Pearl's idea, and it was a good one. Half the men who had taken out their money earlier in the day rushed to put it back." Bonnie's smirk blossomed. "Smart girl, that Pearl. I'm glad I rescued her from—"

"How dare you?" Rex's voice boomed behind Bonnie before she could finish her sentence.

"Papa!" Vivian and Melinda called in unison, then rushed across the porch, past Bonnie, Honoria, and Bebe, to stand by Rex's side as he mounted the top porch step. He'd been approaching through Bonnie's entire speech. Honoria winced. If they hadn't ignored Vivian and Melinda, they would have seen as much.

"You conniving little bitch," Rex seethed, marching to stand towering over Bonnie.

Behind him Rance ambled onto the porch and pinched Vivian's backside. It was a sign of just how absorbed in the scene unfolding in front of her both Vivian and Melinda were that Vivian didn't even flinch.

"I told you she was a wicked woman," Vivian barked. "I've told you all along."

"Stay out of this!" Rex hollered loud enough to make Vivian and Melinda both jump. Rance was there to catch Vivian, and to Honoria's surprise, Vivian cowered in his arms.

That was the least exciting thing going on.

"I treat you like a queen," Rex went on, bellowing at Bonnie. "I shower you with gifts and take you on holidays, and this is how you repay me?"

For her part, Bonnie stood up to Rex with fire in her eyes. "My money is mine to do with as I please."

"It is not *your* money, it is mine!"

"The moment you give it over to my hands, it's mine. That's always been the arrangement between us, Rex. I give, you give, and after that, it's none of your business."

Honoria swallowed the sick lump that formed in her throat. She didn't want to think about what Bonnie gave to her father.

Rex's face had gone red, but he clearly wasn't about to back down. "And where has all this giving led us, woman? You waste my hard-earned money on tarts and trollops and n—s."

Bebe gasped. Honoria flinched at the offensive word and looked away. Whatever shred of respect she'd had left for her father was withering fast.

"It is not a waste of money to buy young girls out of pitiful situations, to give them proper medical care and nutrition, and to educate them," Bonnie argued.

"You run a whorehouse," Rex shouted in return. "You rescue those girls from one bed so they can spread their legs in another."

"Papa, stop!" Melinda clapped her hands to her ears and scrunched her face.

Bonnie's expression resolved into one of calm and power. "Those are only the ones you see, Rex. They're the ones who choose to continue their profession. They make up a fraction of the girls I've rescued."

An odd twist curled through Honoria's stomach. Is that what Bonnie had been doing all these years? Was that why she had never been able to keep track of the girls who worked over at Bonnie's place? How many young women had Bonnie saved…using her father's money? All the respect for her father that Honoria had lost doubled and tripled as it found a new home in Bonnie.

"You'll focus on rescuing yourself if you know what's good for you," Rex railed on, with no sense whatsoever of how much nobler than him Bonnie was.

"And I'm sure you'll tell me how to do that," Bonnie answered, crossing her arms.

"Oooh," Melinda squealed. "Do we have to hear these sorts of things? They're vile, disgusting, and putrid. I'm never, ever, ever going to do any of that with *anybody!*"

Honoria would have rolled her eyes as her sister's newfound streak of prudishness if she wasn't so alarmed by things her father could demand of Bonnie.

But to her surprise, he growled, "I want you to stop resisting and marry me."

Honoria's brow flew up. Bebe's mouth dropped open. Vivian grunted in disgust, and Melinda dropped her hands from her ears long enough to say, "What?"

Bonnie kept her lips pressed firmly shut.

"I am through with you dragging your heels," Rex went on as though his children weren't standing there as witnesses. "No more excuses. You *will* marry me and you *will* produce a son within a year!"

Understanding dawned on Honoria, and she winced. Her father wanted a son. Bonnie was the closest, easiest, and most likely woman to give him that without him having to go out of his way to court. He never had cared to associate with women much. Honoria suspected he couldn't stand most of them. His arrangement with Bonnie had always seemed more like business than pleasure, and now he wanted to take that business to another level.

"You will stop your vain protests and do what you should have done all along and marry me," Rex continued, glaring at Bonnie. "I want that son. I need that son to carry on the Bonneville name and inherit this ranch."

"Hey! What about me?" Rance yelped in protest, shoving Vivian to the side. "Ain't I supposed to do all that?"

Rex clenched his jaw, a vein throbbing in his temple. He whipped around to face Rance. "You have proven to be an even bigger disappointment than my useless daughters."

Vivian and Melinda shrieked in hurt and offense. Bebe merely sagged. Honoria didn't react at all. Her father's pronouncement wasn't a surprise to her.

"That's not… I don't… You can't…" Rance huffed out a breath. "Well, shoot!"

Rex grimaced and snapped back to face Bonnie. "No more games from you! You will marry me and you will have a son, or you will never see another cent from me! How do you think your precious girls would fare then?"

After so much shouting, the silence that fell over the porch was disconcerting. Honoria's back ached with the pain that she could see Bonnie was in. And here she'd thought her problems were bigger than anyone else's. Compared to the situation facing Bonnie, the troubles Honoria had been through were insignificant.

That thought alone made her want to weep. Who was she to play the martyr? She was alive. *Alive*! Alive, healthy, and married to a wonderful, kind man who would never make the kind of vile demands on her that her own father was more than likely to make on Bonnie. She was a fool to have rushed to judgment, assuming Solomon would never forgive her for lying. Right in front of her was what a heartless man who could never forgive looked like. Solomon was not that man, not her father. Once again, she'd made a terrible, foolish mistake.

"I have to go home," she whispered, taking a half step back. "I have to go back to my husband."

"You will stay right there, you stupid wench!" Rex bellowed, pointing to the floor in front of Honoria's feet. "I've endured enough humiliation for one day!"

Rather than being cowed by the force of his anger, Honoria bristled. He may have been her father, but he had no right to speak to her like that. Nothing he could say could make her stay in his house for a second longer than she wanted to.

He evidently thought he'd shouted her into submission, though. He turned his attention back to Bonnie. "What will it be?" he demanded. "Will you marry me or will you go peddle yourself to every slavering scrounger with money in his hand?"

Silence fell again. Bonnie faced Rex with her back straight, but Honoria could feel the weight of the decision before her, the decision that could very well destroy her life. It seemed bitterly unfair, but if there was one thing life had taught her, it was that quite often things were unfair.

"All right," Bonnie answered at last, her voice quiet. "I'll marry you."

"Good," Rex spat. There was no joy in his expression as he got his way. "The wedding will be tomorrow."

"It'll have to wait a couple of weeks," Bonnie countered him.

"What?" Rex's glare was ominous.

"I said, It'll have to wait."

"Why?"

Bonnie shifted her weight to one hip, crossing her arms again. "Do you want to marry me or not?"

"Don't play games with me, woman," Rex threatened.

"Then it will have to wait a couple of weeks."

The two of them stared each other down. Honoria hardly dared to take a breath. It looked like her sisters felt the same way.

At last, Rex hissed out a breath and said, "Fine." He turned away with a sneer. "I've got work to do. You can-"

"Honoria!"

Honoria's heart caught in her throat. She whipped around to look out over the front yard and the drive, everyone else turning to see what it was with her. Joy and terror mingled together in Honoria's chest as she spotted Solomon galloping down the drive toward her.

# Chapter Fifteen

"Solomon!" she called out. The truth of where she belonged and what she needed to do was suddenly so clear that she couldn't have held herself back if she'd tried. She lunged past Bonnie, rushing down the porch stairs to meet her husband as he came for her.

Before her feet could touch the gravel path in front of the stairs, she was grabbed and yanked back. Her feet flew out from under her, and though she twisted painfully, she didn't fall. It took a few disorienting seconds for her to realize her father had her by one arm and Cousin Rance had her by the other.

"Honoria!" Solomon shouted again. He tugged his mount to a stop several yards away and jumped down like a practiced cowboy, in spite of his tailored suit. Hardly taking a moment to gain his footing, he dashed toward her. "Unhand my wife at once!"

"Are you telling *me* what to do, boy?" Rance snapped. He jerked Honoria's arm, but the gesture loosened his hold on her, and she was able to wrench herself free. Her father still held tightly to her other arm, though.

For once, Solomon didn't take the path of calm, silent protest. His eyes flashed with fury and power radiated from him. "If you do not let my wife go this instant, sir, I cannot be held responsible for my actions."

"Let me go, Papa," Honoria seconded, yanking and pulling to get away from him.

"She's mine," Rex snarled. "Always has been, whether you've soiled her with your filthy black paws or not."

"I am not yours," Honoria shouted. She put every last bit of her effort into breaking away from her father.

Whether it was her strength or Rex's shock at her defiance, he let go just as she struggled away. The sudden dizziness of freedom left her stumbling as she lurched forward. Her feet seemed to tangle together, but before she splattered to the path, Solomon was there to catch her.

"Honoria!" His exclamation was filled with more relief than anything else this time. He gathered her into his arms, hugging her tightly as he backpedaled a few steps. "Thank God you're all right."

"I am. I am all right." All at once every emotion that she had kept at bay and every implication of learning she had a long life in front of her hit her. She burst into tears. "I'm not dying, Solomon! I'm so sorry. This is all my fault, and I know you'll never be able to forgive me."

"What is the meaning of this?" Rex shouted, but stayed glued to the stairs. "I want this man removed from my property at once!"

Both his question and his demand were ignored.

"Never be able to forgive you?" Solomon looked as though he had been struck with a brick. "Honoria, learning that you are not dying is the most wonderful piece of news I've ever received."

"Honoria is dying?" Vivian asked from the side of the porch. She leaned against the railing, watching the scene unfold with wide eyes.

"No, she's not," Bebe announced as though she'd staged a coup. "Dr. Abernathy told her the wrong thing. She's not really dying." Bebe looked so proud of knowing what was going on before her sisters that she tilted her chin up with a smug grin.

It lasted until Vivian and Melinda snapped in unison, "Shut up, Bebe!"

Bebe slumped, but her humiliation was quickly overshadowed.

Rex shouted, "Explain this all to me now!"

It was a shock that Honoria didn't have to summon vast amounts of courage to turn to her father and say, "I thought I was sick. I thought my cough was the sign of something worse. So I went to see Dr. Meyers about it."

"How dare you see anyone but Dr. Abernathy without my permission?" Rex growled.

"I saw Dr. Meyers specifically because I didn't want to seek your permission," Honoria blasted him in return. "I am tired of needing your permission to move or think or breathe, especially when you don't care one way or another what I do as long as it doesn't draw attention."

"Why, you impudent—"

"Dr. Meyers ran tests, but he was called out of town before he could deliver the results," Honoria charged on over top of her father. "Your precious Dr. Abernathy was supposed to share the results, but he confused my file with another patient. He told me I have consumption, when in fact I'm perfectly healthy."

"Why would you—"

"I left your house as fast as I could when I thought my time on this earth was short," Honoria raged on, taking a few steps closer to her father. "I begged Solomon to marry me, to keep me safe and to make my last days happy ones. I knew that he was far more capable of making me happy than you ever were."

"Honoria, if you don't cease this foolishness this instant—"

"The only foolishness that I am ceasing is the foolishness of this family," Honoria capped off the last of the things she needed to say. "I am not a Bonneville anymore. I don't think I ever was one. I'm a Templesmith now."

That was it. The beginning and end of everything she had to say. She held her head high and turned to walk back to Solomon.

"Don't you turn your back on me, young lady," Rex boomed.

Honoria didn't pay any more attention to him than she would pay to a fly. Unfortunately for her, she owed far more to the person who did deserve her attention.

"I'm sorry," she repeated, walking until she stood in front of Solomon, her head lowered. "I feel as though I lied to you and forced you to marry me for a reason that doesn't exist. And so much trouble has come because of it."

"Oh, sweetheart," Solomon sighed. Honoria snapped her head up, eyes wide. Solomon rested a hand on the side of her face. "I don't care what your reasons where when you asked me to marry you. I should have had the courage to speak to you and court you long before that."

"I… Really?" She could hardly believe her ears, hardly dared to see the hope and love in Solomon's eyes.

"Of course." He reached for her hands, holding them

tightly to his chest. "I've admired you from afar for years. When you came to me, when you trusted me with something as precious as your final days, I…" He shook his head, unable to find words to express the emotion that was growing bigger and bigger around him. "And then to find out that you're not dying after all?" He burst into laughter and tears at the same time. "I never thought I could be so blessed."

The maelstrom of emotions raging inside of Honoria broke into tears with the force of his reaction. "I couldn't possibly let myself hope," she managed to squeak out, though her whole body was trembling with rapture. "After all the problems I caused, all of the disaster that was because of me…"

"It was nothing, my sweet, wonderful darling wife. Nothing at all." He pulled her into his arms, holding her close. "I would endure it all again and more to be with you for the rest of our long, long lives."

She was too overjoyed to say anything but, "Solomon!" and to throw herself against him. With all her heart, she kissed him, knowing that this was just one of a thousand more kisses to come.

"Disgusting!" Melinda cried out on the porch.

"You'll regret this, you usurping darkie," Rex grumbled.

"Want me to shoot him, Uncle Rex?" Rance asked, though with a large amount of worry that Rex might actually say yes in his voice.

Rex ignored him. "If you think you can get away with this, then you have another thing coming, boy."

With her arms still around him, Honoria could plainly feel the jolt of tension that shot through Solomon. He turned, still clasping her in his arms, to face Rex.

"If you think you can intimidate me with your hollow

threats, you're dead wrong, sir," he declared, back straight, head held high. "You can bully me and undermine my business and my life all you want, but today has shown me that I have friends who will be there when I need them, and that good wins out over evil every time."

"I will not be spoken to that way by the likes of you," Rex hissed.

"You will be spoken to in any way I wish to speak to you," Solomon fired back. "I have earned that right by weathering every storm you've sent in my direction. And if you choose to send more, why, then I'll just take Honoria and go somewhere far beyond your bitter, impotent influence."

"How dare you speak to my papa like that?" Vivian shrieked. "Papa, do something!"

"There's nothing he can do," Honoria bit back at her. "There's nothing a weak man can do when he's met a man who is far superior to him in courage and character."

"Somebody make her stop," Vivian whined, shaking her hands in useless irritation.

"You may hound me," Solomon went on. "You may destroy my business and take all my money, but you can never take Honoria away from me. I might end up without a penny to my name, but I will be the richest man in the world as long as I have my wife by my side." He turned to Honoria with a wide smile. "My beautiful, clever, vibrant wife, who I will love for all of our many, many days."

For a moment Honoria's heart stopped in her chest. "You...you love me?"

Solomon blinked, looking startled at her question. "Of course I do. Didn't you know?"

"No!" She broke out in trembling from head to toe.

"I…I knew you cared for me and that you…that we enjoy each other."

"No, no!" Melinda slapped her hands over her ears again, squeezing her eyes shut. "It's too disgusting. I don't ever even want to think about it!"

"I love you," Solomon said loudly, drowning out Melinda's whine. "I love you more than anything I've ever known."

"And I love you," Honoria was quick to tell him. She hugged him tight, but then leaned back so she could study his handsome, joyful face. "I've loved you for so long. Longer than you could ever guess."

"And we both have so much time ahead of us to love each other," he added, then kissed her soundly.

Somewhere on the edges of her awareness, Honoria heard Melinda squealing again and Vivian making some sort of snide comment. It didn't matter. Bebe was jumping up and down and clapping, and her father had turned to say something low and bitter to Rance, but that didn't matter either. All that mattered was that she was alive, she was in Solomon's arms, and not only was he not angry, he loved her.

When at last she burst through heaven and landed back on earth once more, it was in time to hear Rex growl, "Get off my property, the both of you. I never want to see either of you again."

Honoria took a breath and turned to face her father with defiance. "Well, you'll have to see us, Papa. We live in the same town, and with Solomon's bank on the mend, we're not going anywhere. You can complain about it all you want, but I'm still your flesh and blood, and all of the children Solomon and I have will be your flesh and blood too."

The thought sent Honoria's heart soaring, even

though Rex cursed and spit in the dirt. He didn't even reply. He grabbed Rance by the sleeve and marched away with him.

"Darling, let's go home," Solomon said, taking Honoria's hand. "There's nothing for us here and everything for us back in town."

Honoria smiled like she had never smiled before and leaned into him for another kiss. She turned to go with him, but at the last minute gasped and turned back.

"Bonnie," she called to her friend.

Bonnie was watching them with a sad smile, but blinked and stood straighter at her name. "What?"

"Come back to town. You don't have to marry Papa. I'm sure we can figure out how to finance your efforts on behalf of the girls."

Solomon sent Honoria a confused and gently wary look.

Bonnie must have seen it. She sighed and shook her head. "I've made my bed, honey. It's about time I lay in it."

"But—"

"Nope. It's already decided." Bonnie cut her off before she could say more. "I knew this day would come, and I accept it as the price I must pay."

"Ugh, she's so melodramatic," Vivian snorted. She grabbed Melinda's arm and turned to go inside. Before they took more than a few steps, Vivian turned to Bebe. "Bebe! Come! Now!"

A stricken Bebe looked between Vivian and Honoria, at a complete loss.

"Bebe!" Melinda added her command to her sisters.

"If you ever need me, I'll be there for you," Honoria told Bebe.

Still looking miserable, Bebe nodded, then scurried after Vivian and Melinda.

"She'll take you up on that offer in time," Bonnie sighed.

"Will you take me up on it too?" Honoria asked.

Bonnie shook her head. She didn't say anything more except, "You two go on before your father takes it into his head to do something stupider than he's already done."

Hard though it was, Honoria accepted Bonnie's choice. She squeezed Solomon's hand. Together they turned and walked back to his horse. Solomon helped her to mount, then climbed up behind her.

"I meant what I said," he insisted as he reached around her waist for the reins. "I would happily lose everything else now that I have you."

She twisted to face him as well as she could, laying a hand on the side of his face, "And I would gladly die if it meant that you could be happy."

He laughed. "Lucky for us, we don't have to worry about that for years to come."

# *Epilogue*

It's strange the way life works. It was only two weeks later that Honoria was back in Dr. Meyers's office, being examined once more.

"Are you certain your original diagnosis was right?" Solomon asked, pacing the tiny space to the side of the examination table where Dr. Meyers worked.

"I'm certain," Dr. Meyers, chuckled. How he could be so light-hearted when she was feeling so poorly was beyond Honoria.

"We can't be too careful," Solomon went on. "I've already experienced the pain of thinking I was going to lose my wife once. I'm not in a hurry to do it again."

"Well, you're in luck." Dr. Meyers helped Honoria to sit up, then stepped back from the table. "It's early days still, but I think I can make a definitive diagnosis as to Honoria's condition."

Honoria's heart sank. "It's the strain of making a break with my family, isn't it?" she blurted. "It was so traumatic, and I've been so tired and nauseated since then."

Dr. Meyers hummed and tilted his head to the side. "It does have something to do with family."

Solomon let out a heavy breath and rubbed a hand over his face. "I've been working hard on finding forgiveness for that lot, but so help me, if they take my darling Honoria away from me again…"

"It's not that." Dr. Meyers continued to chuckle.

Honoria wasn't sure she was in the mood to listen to someone who should know better behave so callously at such a serious time. "Then what is it?" she asked.

"I know Rex Bonneville is mighty keen to have a son," Dr. Meyers went on. "But it looks like he's going to end up with a grandson—or granddaughter—before that."

"If he thinks—" Solomon started, but stopped flat a second later. His mouth dropped open and his eyes went wide.

The news took Honoria completely by surprise as well. At the same time, she knew instantly that it was true.

"A baby!" She exclaimed. "But…but we've only been married for a little over a month."

Dr. Meyers shrugged. "Not to be indelicate, but as long as the two of you are enjoying a normal, healthy marriage, it is very possible for a baby to come along so soon."

Solomon laughed and slapped Dr. Meyers on the back. "I wouldn't say our marriage has been normal, exactly. But you're right, a baby is possible."

"Not just possible," Honoria said, hopping off the table. "It's factual. We're having a baby!" She rushed into Solomon's arms, barely able to believe how blessed she was. One minute she'd been certain she was going to die, and the next she was about to bring a new life into the world.

"Now, there are still complications that can occur,"

Dr. Meyers went on as if delivering a speech he was honor-bound to share. "But Honoria is extremely healthy, as we all now know, and in the prime of her child-bearing years. I think this pregnancy will proceed without trouble."

He gave them more information and made sure they knew what they needed to do, both for Honoria's health and for the health of the baby. Afterwards, both equally stunned, Honoria and Solomon headed out of Dr. Meyers's office and down Prairie Avenue toward Station Street in a daze.

"We're going to be a family," Solomon spoke at last, hugging Honoria's arm tightly as he escorted her.

"We're already a family," Honoria giggled. She couldn't seem to stop herself once she got going. "I hope we do have a boy," she went on. "It would be grand to nurture a little Solomon, Jr. as he grew to be a fine banker, like his father."

Solomon laughed. "I think I'd rather like to have an Honoria, Jr. if it's all the same."

Honoria swatted at his arm, her heart so light she thought she might float. "If it is a girl, can we name her Ariana? After my mother."

A fond smile spread across Solomon's handsome face, made even more handsome by pure bliss and contentment. "Ariana Templesmith. I think I like it."

They continued on in a cloud of delight, walking arm in arm as if the world didn't matter. The only thing that threatened to upset the perfection of the moment was the sight of Bonnie fussing with a carpetbag as she waited on the platform of Haskell's train station. She was dressed in full travel regalia, complete with gloves and a veiled hat.

"Bonnie!" Honoria let go of Solomon's arms and rushed over to the edge of the platform.

"Take it easy, Sweetheart," Solomon called after her.

Honoria was certain that was the first of many ways that Solomon would wrap her up in cotton-wool during her pregnancy, but at the moment, she had bigger concerns. "Are you running away at last?" she asked, stepping up onto the train platform and taking Bonnie's hands. "Thank God!"

"No." Bonnie laughed, though there wasn't much humor in it. "Just taking a short trip."

"Where?" Honoria blinked, confused. Solomon stepped up to the platform and walked to her side, resting a hand on the small of her back.

"To Everland," Bonnie explained.

"Everland?" Solomon frowned. "Whatever for?"

Bonnie sighed. "I told Rex I had something I had to take care of before I could marry him."

"And it's in Everland?" Honoria asked.

Bonnie nodded.

"Whatever is it?" Solomon followed.

The corner of Bonnie's mouth twitched with mischief and something Honoria couldn't quite name.

"Before I can marry your father, I've got to divorce my husband."

Yes, I can hear you right now, "Whaaaaaaaaat? Bonnie is already married? When? How? Who? What's going on?" Yes, it's true. Because historically speaking, not all mail-order bride stories worked out back in the days of the Old West. The law wasn't always around to help people cut ties legally either. But sometimes, if people let enough water run under the bridge, old misunderstandings could be mended. One little trip to Everland might give Bonnie and a certain Rupert Cole a second chance to fall in love. Be sure to find out in late October in *His Secret Bride*!

If you haven't checked out the Everland series by Caroline Lee, you might just want to do that before *His Secret Bride*! The Everland series starts with *Ella*, and you can get your first glimpse of Rupert Cole in book two, *Little Red*!

# About the Author

I hope you have enjoyed *His Forbidden Bride*. If you'd like to be the first to learn about when new books in the series come out and more, please sign up for my newsletter here: http://eepurl.com/RQ-KX And remember, Read it, Review it, Share it! For a complete list of works by Merry Farmer with links, please visit http://wp.me/P5ttjb-14F.

Merry Farmer is an award-winning novelist who lives in suburban Philadelphia with her two cats, Butterfly and Torpedo. She has been writing since she was ten years old and realized one day that she didn't have to wait for the teacher to assign a creative writing project to write something. It was the best day of her life. She then went on to earn not one but two degrees in History so that she would always have something to write about. Her books have topped the Amazon and iBooks charts and have been named finalists in the prestigious RONE and Rom Com Reader's Crown awards.

You can email her at merryfarmer20@yahoo.com or follow her on Twitter @merryfarmer20.
Merry also has a blog, http://merryfarmer.net,
and a Facebook page,
www.facebook.com/merryfarmerauthor

# Acknowledgements

I owe a huge debt of gratitude to my awesome beta-readers, Caroline Lee, Carly Cole, and Jolene Stewart, for their suggestions and advice. And a big, big thanks to my editor, Cissie Patterson, for doing an outstanding job, as always, and for leaving hilarious comments throughout the manuscript. Also, a big round of applause for my marketing and promo mistress, Sara Benedict.

And a special thank you to the Pioneer Hearts group! Do you love Western Historical Romance? Wanna come play with us? Become a member at https://www.facebook.com/groups/pioneerhearts/

# Other Series by Merry Farmer

**The Noble Hearts Trilogy**
(Medieval Romance)

**Montana Romance**
(Historical Western Romance – 1890s)

**Hot on the Trail**
(Oregon Trail Romance – 1860s)

**The Brides of Paradise Ranch –**
**Spicy and Sweet Versions**
(Wyoming Western Historical Romance – 1870s)

Willow: Bride of Pennsylvania
(Part of the American Mail-Order Brides series)

**Second Chances**
(contemporary romance)

The Advisor
(Part of The Fabulous Dalton Boys trilogy)

**The Culpepper Cowboys**
(Contemporary Western - written in partnership with
Kirsten Osbourne)

**New Church Inspiration**
(Historical Inspirational Romance – 1880s)

**Grace's Moon**
(Science Fiction)

41441820R00134

Made in the USA
Middletown, DE
13 March 2017